Tales of the Restoration

David and Karen Mains

Interior illustrations by Linda Wells

Cook Communications

Cook Communications Ministries,
Colorado Springs, Colorado 80918
Cook Communications, Paris, Ontario
Kingsway Communications, Eastbourne, England

Designed by Jeff Lane
Cover illustration by Rob Grist

First hardcover printing, 1996
First printing of paperback edition, 2000
Printed in Canada
04 03 02 01 00 5 4 3 2 1

Library of Congress Cataloging-in-Publication Data

Mains, David R.
Tales of the Restoration / written by David and Karen Mains ; interior illustrations by Linda Wells.
p. cm.
Sequel to: Tales of the Resistance.
Summary: The residents of Bright City continue the struggle to subdue evil and to restore the King and his bride as their rulers.
ISBN 0-7814-3289-8
[1. Fantasy.] I. Mains, Karen Burton. II. Wells, Linda, ill. III. Title.

PZ7.M2782 Tas 2000
[Fic]—dc21 99-087659

TABLE OF CONTENTS

Grandma Vigilantes

"*Wh-e-e-e-et! Wh-e-e-e-et!*" The whistle sounded softly in the thick darkness of the night. Grandma Sarah woke instantly, the warning signal jolting her from slumber.

"*Wh-e-e-e-et! Wh-e-e-e-et!*" Few heard the call. But those whose ears were trained turned in their beds, shook off the covers, and made ready to do battle. The warning meant that dark things were creeping out of the Garbage

Dump to do damage somewhere. Danger had breached the Surround that protected Bright City.

"Wh-e-e-e-et! Wh-e-e-e-et!" It was the whistle for the Grandma Vigilantes.

Grandma Sarah dressed quickly in the deepest-of-midnight blue pants, which she yanked up over her wrinkled legs and then, with one more tug, up far above her waist. Over her head she pulled a matching cable knit sweater for warmth. Tucking her white hair beneath a knit stocking cap, she tied the laces on solid black shoes with thick flat heels. Double knots—no need tripping while on the streets. She patted her pants pockets. Yes, there was a big box of strikes.

Careful to keep her balance, she strapped around her left knee the most important weapon of all, her ever ready beeper. Steadying herself with a sturdy walking cane in her right hand, she cautiously touched that knee to the ground, setting off the beeper. She bowed her head closely to listen. *Bz-z-z-z-z-z. Bz-z-z-z-z-z.* Ah, good! The battery was still strong, the signal low but clear. She was ready to take her place on night patrol.

Grandpa Daniel still lay in bed, snoring and deep in sleep. Grandma Sarah pulled the covers over his chin and whispered a blessing over his dreams. "To the King!" Then she tiptoed from the bedroom, from the house, to where her patrol partner should be waiting on the street outside. With Kingsways she would be gone and back before dawnsbreak, back before her husband even woke and had a chance to worry.

On the front porch, Grandma Sarah touched her left knee to the ground and tapped out a secret code: two short buzzes and one long. *Bz-bz-bzzzzz.* This meant: *Grandma Vigilante reporting for patrol. Are you there?* One could never be too careful on the streets at night. In the dark, all shadows looked alike.

The answer came back, a quick code in reverse: *Bzzzz-bz-bz.* This meant: *Grandma Vigilante reporting. Yes, I am here.* A tall, thin form stepped from behind a lamppost. Ah, good, Ruthie was near and ready. The two were longtime partners on night patrol.

By day these grandmas (and hundreds of others, two for every block) were gray-haired ladies with slightly stooped backs, or soft comfy tummies, or saggy arms, or wrinkled faces. In daylife all were grannies who doted on their grandchildren. They said, "Of course, dear," to their husbands. They baked endless batches of walnut chip molasses cookies and kept their houses in immaculate order. But at night, when their grandpa husbands were sleeping from a full day of labor for the Restoration, at night when danger was most near, when Naysayers or Burners or Breakers dared to invade the City of the King, slipping through cracks in the holy Surround, then these grannies became (who would have thought it?) the fierce Grandma Vigilantes!

The grandma patrols, moving stealthily two by two, looked like aging cat burglars and might be laughable to some. But the Enchanter's legions had learned to fear their blitz attacks and no longer took any old ladies for granted. The dark things had learned that when danger threatened grandchildren, these grannies showed no mercy. They took no prisoners, they scorned negotiations. Their canes were deadly and their deep-knee bends proved lethal to the cause of the Enchanter.

"So, Ruthie, what's going down tonight?" whispered Grandma Sarah, pausing in the street to pull dark gloves over her gnarled fingers. When they had finished their night disguises, the old women linked the hooks of their canes so as not to become separated in the darkness.

"Oh, dearie, the worst of the worst is out tonight," muttered Grandma Ruth. "There are Sleepstealers on the prowl."

"Those low-down dirty crawlers. Stealing beautiful dreams! They hate it when the City rests at night and lives in daylife. Well, we'll fix 'em, won't we, Ruthie?"

"Sure gonna try, Sarah, sweetie." And the tall, thin granny chuckled under her breath. Despite the danger, the two were too old to be afraid. They had worked for the Restoration for a long time, and they knew the secret: those who practiced deep-knee bends at night became filled with Kingspower.

Grandma Sarah went to bend her knee, and Grandma Ruth steadied her elbow, "Careful, dearie. Remember the arthritis." The buzzer emitted two long signals: *Bz-z-z-z-z-z. Bz-z-z-z-z-z. We are on the vigil. Who is keeping vigil too?*

Throughout the city, her signal was answered. *Bz-z-z-z-z-z. Bz-z-z-z-z-z: We are on the vigil. Who is keeping vigil with us?*

From the sound of the many echoing buzzers, it seemed that Grandma Vigilantes were out in force. Sleepstealers were abroad, and following them for sure were the Naysayers. The first went creeping and stealing the good dream stories, and the second came sneaking behind, blowing bad tales into the ears of sleeping boys and girls, men and women.

From somewhere down the street, the two patrol partners heard a soft toot, *"Harnk! Harnk!"* They paused, still joined by their cane handles, waiting for a MERCY ST. TAXI CORPS cab to loom out of the darkness.

Once, before the King had freed the people of the city from nightlife, the City Taxi Co. had been the underground headquarters for the Resistance. But after Burning Place, after New Day's Rising, the valiant company had been renamed and now dedicated itself to aiding the work of the Restoration. It was MERCY ST. TAXI CORPS that sounded the nighttime warning whistle to waken the Grandma Vigilantes.

"Hey, bubs," growled a gruff whisper.

The two grandmas winked at each other. Sure enough, they had recognized the voice of Pete the cabman. They could just make out the form of his taxi, parked at the curb with the motor purring.

"Evening, young fella," they answered.

"Yes'm, ladies. We got trouble t'night. Them power-outs are doing us no favors. No'm. The creeps been night crawling for sure. Getch'a breach in the Surround and getch'a trouble. That's for sure. Got canes?"

The grandmas nodded.

"Got workin' batteries?"

They nodded again.

Suddenly, a child's cry pierced the night. The sound wrenched their hearts.

Pete growled. "See whad I mean? Got kids screaming with bad night tales all over the city." A red light blinked on the dashboard, and the cabby shifted gears. "Yep. Yep. Look here. Something is cornered. Gotta give some grannies a hand." The taxi started away, the tires squealed, the brake lights flashed, stopped, backed up. Pete called, "Oh, forgot to ask. Think you ladies can handle your patrol without me for a while?"

They took his neglect as a compliment to their fighting skills, nodded, and shooed him along. The tires squealed again, and this time, the cab-man did not come back. Stretching their linked canes out to full length, Grandma Sarah and Grandma Ruth began their patrol stroll. They slowly semi-circled down the sidewalk, the motion of the arc propelling each granny out and forward by turn.

"Handsome young fella, isn't he, Ruthie?"

"A real nice boy," agreed Ruth, then whispered, "See anything?"

Whereas Grandma Sarah's hearing was a little lacking, her nightsight was superb. "No," she answered in an undertone. "Nothing yet. You hear anything?"

And whereas Grandma Ruth's farsight was a little blurred, her hearing was excellent. The two stood still, one listening, one staring; they heard nothing and started the patrol stroll again.

"Ee-ee-ee-ee-ee!" A child's scream pierced the silent night.

"If I get my hands on a Sleepstealer, he's gonna be real sorry—"

"Sh-h-h-h-h, sweetie." Ruth lifted her hand in warning. "What's that?"

Grandma Sarah stood still, straining to hear.

"Down on your knee! Quick! Down on your knee!"

Without argument, Sarah bent her left knee, trusting to Ruth's unerring ear.

"We got a signal coming from somewhere. Double signal! *Bz-z-z-z-z-z! bz-z-z-z-z!* Double trouble. Sound the triple!"

Grandma Sarah held tightly onto Grandma Ruth's hand for balance. Drat these aches and pains. She pressed her knee to the ground in quick taps; one, two, three. *Bz-z-z-z! bz-z-z-z! bz-z-z-z!* Again: *Bz-z-z-z! bz-z-z-z! bz-z-z-z!* This meant: *Help is near. Where are you?*

From down the block, but close enough, came the answering signal; one long sustained buzzer that another nearby patrol could track. *Bz-z-z-z-z-z-z-z-z-z-z-z-z-z-z-z-z-z.* This meant: *Follow quickly.* The two grannies hastened, because everyone knew that the danger with a long deep-knee buzzer was that anything, good or bad, could follow its signal.

Grandma Sarah and Grandma Ruth linked elbows and hurried toward the emergency call. Staying together, they peered into doorways and lit strikes, the tiny flashes of fire that blazed to light alleys and cul-de-sacs where Burners and Breakers liked to hide.

"Stop!" whispered Grandma Sarah. Her sharp eyes had detected motion—something shadowy flitting around the corner of a building. "This way. Use the hobble-cobble."

Ruth could see nothing, but she trusted her partner's nightsight.

Then there was a sudden silence. The long follow-quickly signal had abruptly stopped.

The two grandmas hooked their canes again, spread them to full length, and began to march; outside legs forward and together—Hobble! Inside legs forward and together—Cobble! Outside legs forward and together—Hobble! Inside legs forward and together—Cobble! Their thick heels clunked noisily. Hobble-cobble-clunk-clunk! Hobble-cobble-clunk-clunk! As one stretching unit they turned the corner of the nearby building, sweeping anything shadowy before them.

Sure enough. A whole circle of dark shadows was inching closer and closer to another form huddled in the courtyard of a housing complex. Dark things—and it looked like—oh, my gracious, it looked like a solo granny.

"Halt! Who goes there?" cried Grandma Ruth.

Then, without waiting for an answer, the two women chanted in one voice, "In the Name of the King, the Most High One, the Day Bringer, the Lord of Light, we command you to cease and desist."

Here in this courtyard, in the night, their words began to call forth Ranger protection, to knit together some hole that had opened in the Surround. That would hold them for a few minutes. The shadows stopped advancing upon the lonely granny.

Grandma Ruth took several strikes from her pants pocket. She flicked them with her thumbnail, they flared. She threw them into the air, they gave off sudden light. "Well, my, my, my, Sarah sweetie. What have we here?"

Grandma Sarah's sharp sight scouted the shadows, "I'd say we've got a handful of Burners and Breakers, a patrol granny alone (of all things), and a couple of Naysayers for good measure. And lookee here, we've got a sure enough Sleepstealer climbing up a drainpipe."

"That dirty night crawler. Tsk-tsk-tsk. Meanness just shouldn't be allowed. Think we can handle this bunch, Ruthie, or should we signal for Pete?"

"Ah, that young fella's busy. Don't we usually end up helping him anyway? We can handle this bunch. But first let's brace up that solo granny."

She called out: "Granny! Granny! Don't be afraid. You are no longer alone. Remember the Rule: Fear always lets the dark things near. Do you have your handbag?"

The granny in the center of the courtyard stopped huddling against the wall. She clutched her bag to her ample bosom. Recalling her vigilante training, she quickly began calling out the Litany of Names, "His Majesty . . . our Sovereign Liege Lord . . . His Eminence . . . the Benevolent Potentate . . ."

As if to drown out her words, a counter-chant began from the shadows, "Nay. Nay. Nay-nay-nay." Then louder: "NAY. NAY. NAY-NAY-NAY!"

"Well, wouldn't you know?" said Grandma Ruth. "Always got a pack of Naysayers around if they can sniff out fear."

Grandma Sarah began to unscrew her secret weapon, the handle crook from the stem of her cane. "Shall we take out the Sleepstealer first? Before he creeps in that open window?"

"Good idea," said Ruthie, "and better be quick about it." Her sharp ears were picking up the sounds of shuffling feet somewhere in the courtyard.

Grandma Sarah looped her loosened handle crook around the end of the cane stem. She held both out and above her head, circling the crook, now an instant boomerang, round and round. "In the head or between the shoulder blades, Ruthie?"

"Don't be nice! Give the meanie a good knock on the noggin'." Grandma Ruth flicked a strike for quick light.

Grandma Sarah let fly. The cane crook went whizzing round and round, a high-pitched whine screeching as it wanged through the air: *Scre-e-e-e-e-e-e-e-e-e-tch; tch; tch; tch; tch.* It clunked the Sleepstealer directly on the back of the head, knocking him down the drainpipe. The pipe tore away from the wall, it teetered back and forth, back and forth. The Sleepstealer kicked and scrambled with his feet in midair, holding on for dear life. "Whoa-a-a-a-a-a!" The pipe leaned low, lower and lower, then sprang back, striking the wall and shaking the intruder to the ground where he rolled into a hump.

"Duck, grannies!" Ruth cried as the crook boomeranged back.

Sarah lifted her cane tip to hook it in flight.

"NOW!" cried Ruth to the solo granny. "Whack 'em with your bag! Whack 'em all hard!" And at this, the solo granny against the wall began wailing and flailing against the shadows. She made a break for it and joined the other two in the middle of the courtyard.

Grandma Sarah shouted a stroll patrol cry: "CANE WAR! WHUMPING AND THUMPING!" With that, she bent her left knee to the ground and lowered her head to monitor its low steady signal. Better get a back-up just in case.

The two other grandmas linked themselves together by the hooks of their canes, made a circle, and cried back, "CANE WARS!" Sarah stood straight and joined them in the three-way hobble-cobble. Rounding and rounding, they advanced upon the dark things. Hobble-cobble! Clunk-clunk-clunk! Hobble-cobble-clunk-clunk! The shadows edged back, pressed hard against the wall.

Trapped, the Breakers lifted their cudgels and made fierce faces. The Burners pointed their glaring pokers at the advancing grannies. The Naysayers doubled their doomtones. Any other city folk might have trembled, sweat, and fled. But not these three. All three shouted as in one voice, "WHUMPING AND THUMPING!"

With the dark things all trapped against the wall, the grandmas proceeded to take their canes and thrash the shadows. "WHUMP! TAKE THAT! AND THAT!"

Whining, the dark things turned and hid their heads in their hands. "It's his fault," one cried. "Hit him!"

"No!" shouted another. "He's to blame. Whump him!"

"THUMP!" cried Granny Sarah. "That's for making little Jed afraid of the dark."

"TAKE THAT!" cried Granny Ruth. "That's for stealing the safe sleep of tiny Lorena."

"TAKE THAT AND THAT! You are all deserving of whumping!"

As the grannies continued to wallop their enemies' backsides, the lump that had fallen from the drainpipe stirred itself and began to shimmy on its stomach toward the combat, unseen by the battling grannies.

How dare the shadowy things bring danger to Bright City? No mercy! WHUMP! How dare they creep through the fault lines? How dare they steal the good stories from the grandchildren's' dreams? A cudgel flew into the air, then a poker. And the shadowy lump on the floor of the courtyard shimmied closer and closer. Unseen, it grasped a red hot poker. Unseen, it drew itself to its knees at the back of the grannies, and lifted the weapon above its head to strike a blow.

"Dearie! Behind you!" called Grandma Sarah, ducking quickly into a deep knee bend, her head low again to monitor the beeper's signal.

Grandma Ruth turned and took her cane to the Sleepstealer who was creeping up to bash her. "Aha! Gotcha!" she cried and mashed him in the midsection with her cane.

"Mercy. . ." he gasped.

And all three grannies lifted their voices and chanted, "No mercy!" WHUMP! "No prisoners!" THUMP! "No negotiations!"

"Wh-e-e-e-et! HARNK! Wh-e-e-e-et! HARNK!" A taxi screeched into the courtyard. It was Pete. "Grannies! Grannies!" he called. "A'ten-hup!"

The two battling grannies paused from whumping, turned around, and lifted their canes in salute. Grandma Sarah stood to her feet. The buzzing stopped.

Pete the cabman scrambled out, "Good work, grannies. Good battling job!" He opened the back door and barked, "Awright, dark things. Night's almost over. Back to the Garbage Dump with you."

The shadows shuffled about nervously but made no move.

"Or do you prefer the grannies?"

Pushing and shoving, they rushed together as one into the back seat, slamming the cab door behind them.

The Grandma Vigilantes remembered their training: Give no evil in return for evil. They tucked their canes under their arms. They hiked their pants above their waists and stood at attention. "Just in time, young fella," said Grandma Sarah. "I guess we grannies were getting a little—oh, what shall we say—frisky? We've just plumb had it with Sleepstealers."

"Good job, grannies," said Pete. "And solo lady . . . I betcha don't hit the streets alone again. Patrol in twos or you lose."

The solo grandma mumbled something about her partner oversleeping and thinking she could handle it by herself and with the power-outs and everything she thought . . . but hearing her own words, she finally lowered her eyes.

Pete winked at her and said, "Oh, well. Everyone's gotta learn sooner or later that a vigilante rule is a good rule." He slammed the door to the back seat of the taxi and double barred the locks.

"All in a night's work, Petey," smiled Grandma Ruth. "Say, lookee, girls. It's almost dawnbreak." A faint line of light streaked the sky. Morning was always the all-clear signal to night battles. The taxi squealed its tires, tooted the horn softly, *Harnk!,* and sped away.

"Yes," said Grandma Sarah, "Better get back home before Grandpa Daniel wakes up and wonders where I am."

The three grannies stood in the street. They listened to the sounds of Bright City. Ah, that was good. No more childcries. No more night screams. Everyone was dreaming the best of the good story dreams, the ones that came close to morning.

"I guess," said Grandma Sarah as they took off their gloves, shook their hair out from under the discarded knit caps, and strolled toward home. "I guess I'll make a batch of walnut chip molasses cookies today."

The three grannies linked elbows and patrol-strolled with a little dance step down the middle of the empty street. Yes, indeed, despite close calls, it had been a good night's work. "To the Kingdom! To the King!" they said in parting. And each went her separate way to live out her ordinary granny life. But each was proud in her deepest heart, despite loss of sleep, despite danger and difficulty, despite today's aches and pains, to be part of the few, the happy few who kept vigil while the city was deep in sleep.

Crossing Alone

A boy, no longer a child but not yet a man, his narrow shoulders hunched against the night air, waited at the edge of the Garbage Dump for dawn. Little Child's time had come to risk Crossing, and he was cold. He flexed his fingers. He jogged in place. He tried to ignore the fear flip-flopping in his stomach.

Where was the Princess Amanda? wondered Little Child. Why was she taking so long? And how did she get the courage to make Crossing so often, to go back and forth from Great Park to Bright City?

The Garbage Dump was a dangerous place. Though the Enchanted City had been freed by the King from the curse of nightlife, and though the people now lived daylives and called their home Bright City, here in the awful place of ashes and rotting refuse the Naysayers, the Burners, and Breakers still hunted. Here they ambushed crossers who bravely worked for the Restoration. At Day's End, shadows began to creep out of hidey-holes and from behind garbage mounds to breach the city walls and the protection of the Ranger Surround. To make havoc, these dark ones had to work quickly and with deceits, because in day their powers waned. So they cursed each dawnwake and exulted when sunsleep dimmed the skies.

Br-r-r-r. Little Child blew on his fingers. He hummed a tune from Great Celebration to bolster himself against his own fear. He checked his survival kit. Nose masks to protect against poison air. A silver-handled hatchet for battle. Bread and water for one day's journey.

Oh, he wished he could be like his older brother. If only—if only he could have fought beside Hero in the War of Great Park or with the underground fighters in the Time of Resistance. If only he, too, could have chronicled Sightings of the King. He would have endured being a horrified witness at Burning Place for the glory of having seen the King rise laughing from the ashes in a fiery rosy wonder. Little Child wished he could have danced in the first Celebration of the New Day Rising.

But no, he had been too small, and slow growing at that, and assigned to Mercie's care. True, she and he had saved many lost babies in the Great Park Nursery. True too, he had become a skilled babykeeper. But babykeeping had everything to do with kindness and nothing to do with boldness. The thought of the narrow path through the Garbage Dump, the idea of pit-traps and hidden bog-mires made him long for the song of the teakettle and the warmth of the fire. He sighed. He just had to face it: He was no hero.

Little Child crouched on his haunches and huddled for warmth. It was hard being the younger brother of a brave freedom fighter. Oh, he wished he didn't have to make Crossing alone. But the Rule determined: "Only those brave enough to make Crossing by themselves are ready to work in the Restoration with others."

In the dim light, he could just make out the words chiseled in the stone arch above the gate at his back: WELCOME ALL WHO HUNT. At last, day was coming. Tendrils of smoke could be seen curling from the hovels of the No-People who hid in the mounds of decaying refuse. Over this desecrated wasteland, a purple line of light jagged between earth and sky, like an ominous scar on the coming day.

More than anything, more even than his pulsing fear, Little Child wanted to work in the Restoration. "To the Kingdom," he whispered to himself for comfort. "To the King."

Little Child saw a puff of dust unscrolling far down the narrow path before him. He stood to his feet and narrowed his gaze. A figure, still distant, came to sight. If it was the princess, he would soon hear her laughter. She was of the wind and air, of the liveliness of growing things, of the shining sun and the greening earth. Always she came back to Great Park with gladness, having made the dangerous circuit once again unharmed. Was this Amanda? Ah, yes. There was the clear laugh.

"L.C.!" she called. "L.C.! I'm coming! I'm coming!" Breathlessly, a tall young woman reached Stonegate Entrance, grabbed the boy to stop her flight, then whirled them both round and round. "Oh, L.C.! L.C.!" She called him by the nickname she herself had given him years before. "Today you make Crossing! I'm so proud of you. All your friends in Bright City can't wait for you to arrive. Hero said to hurry."

Despite his fears, Little Child laughed to see her. Yet when he tried to talk, his tongue tangled. The moment he had been dreading was upon him. Amanda had crossed at night, risking peril to scout the path. He must return now by himself. "Is . . . is it a bad Crossing today? Is . . . is it a particularly bad Crossing?"

The Princess Amanda had stopped her turning. Her hair was wild and fell in wind-tumbled tangles. Her cheeks were flushed and high with color. She wore the royal-blue running garments of a Restoration Worker with the silver insignia of loyalty embroidered high on her left shoulder. On her feet were dusty felt boots. Her eyes sparkled, blue as cornflowers in July sunshine. But at his question, she held the boy at arm's length to look at him seriously. "L.C., you can't doubt that you are ready. Doubting only makes it worse. Besides, Mercie and

Caretaker say you are ready. And Hero is impatient, asking for you every day."

"I . . . I only want to know what I might be facing. Is it a particularly difficult Crossing?"

Amanda put her arm around the boy's shoulder. She pulled him near her side, and together they faced the Garbage Dump. Beyond that, showing gray and sleepy through the morning mists, stood the Bright City. "I can only tell you that it is not the most difficult Crossing today, but it is not the easiest one either." She dropped her hand from the boy's shoulder and smiled directly at him. Early light was fully upon them. "Hurry now. If it becomes a particularly bad Crossing, you will need the whole day so that you will not be in the wasteland when night comes. The Rules," she demanded. "Repeat to me all Caretaker's Crossing Rules."

Little Child clicked his heels to attention, lifted his chin, and repeated the Rules. "One: Always stay on the path. Do not take any shortcuts or detours. Two: Remember that although you are traveling alone, you are not really alone. Three: Use your greatest gift while Crossing. Four: The path will always show itself if you wait. Five: Only those brave enough to make Crossing alone are ready to work for the Restoration with others."

Smiling brightly, the princess saluted quickly, then walked toward Stonegate Entrance. The iron gate opened before her. When she was beneath the arch, she called back, "Hurry! Don't delay!" and she was gone. Little Child faced the Garbage Dump. He forced himself toward whatever awful unknowns were ahead. Alone.

The path before him led deep into the very heart of the Dump. Mounds of rotting garbage were heaped high and stretched far as the eye could see. Ugly black flies gorged on the refuse. Even in early morning the air felt hot. Piles of castoff machines and broken things and discarded belongings and moldering cloths made places for dark things to hide.

The boy had not gone far before he was out of sight of the entrance. The polluted air stank in his nostrils. He covered his nose with a breathing mask. As he followed the way around a mountain of disgusting garbage, his heart suddenly leaped. Not far, but off the path was a rusting pickup truck, and sitting in it an old man who looked exactly like Caretaker.

"L.C.!" he called. "L.C.! Mercie and I are concerned about you making this Crossing alone. Come. I know all the shortcuts. We will drive the rest of the way together."

Oh, Little Child was glad. He wanted to shout. Now he would quickly see his friends. He would have a safe and easy Crossing and soon be in Bright City with his brother. He stepped off the path and hurried toward the truck—but a question nagged inside. Would Caretaker break his own rules? "Always stay on the path," he had said.

No. No, Caretaker would not break his own rules. Little Child tore himself from his longing for an easy journey, ran back to the path, and raced on as fast as he could go.

A chilling laugh tripped his going: *"Owa-ha-ha; owa-ha-ha. . . ."*

Looking back, he saw the old man rise, tear off a disguise, and uncover the chalk-white face, the smirking grin of a Breaker.

Shaking an ugly knobbed and brutal club over his head, the dark thing laughed again, *"Owa-ha-ha; owa-ha-ha. . . ."*

Little Child shivered at the sight; he was in for it now. Because of breaking the Rule, this not-the-most-difficult of Crossings was liable to become particularly-difficult. Sure enough, somewhere from the middle of the Dump a dull drum started to pound—*Boom! Boom! Boom!*

The Breaker shouted, taunting him. "Nha-nha-na-na-nha-na! You stepped off the path!" The drum again: *Boom! Boom! Boom!* A signal. Now all the dark things at hidden checkpoints would know he was coming, and that he was weak, and that he could be fooled by deceits.

Little Child's heart pounded hard. He had only started, and already he had almost failed. He bolstered his going by humming the Hymn of Courage. He was woefully off-tune, but the sound of the hymn, even without the words, steadied him a little. On he struggled, one foot in front of the other, as the minutes slowly turned into hours.

By midday high, the wretched place had filled him with despair. He struggled up a putrid mountain of refuse he had been climbing for what felt like an hour. Five steps up, a slithering slide back. Forward. Back. Forward. Would he ever get out of here?

Little Child looked around. He could see neither Great Park behind him or Bright City before. But he could still hear the drums. He could still remember the haunting laugh of the Breaker. Suddenly, a terrible howl stopped him in his slipping tracks: *A-a-roo! A-a-roo!* Cautiously he crested the top of the garbage mound. He ripped off the nose mask and, panting hard from the long climb, he looked down. A pack of wild wolves, yapping and slathering, waited below, pacing to and fro across the path. Some lifted on hind legs to peer over the rest, but all the fierce heads were turned up toward him.

Overwhelmed with terror, Little Child ducked low, turned to hide, pressed his spine hard against the back ridge of the hill. How could he possibly follow the path through the middle of those wild beasts? He noticed a sign beside him, its letters faded by smoke and weather: "DETOURS. WOLVES AHEAD." Then in smaller letters printed beneath these, he could just make out, "Friends of Crossers Assoc." A two-headed arrow, split in half, pointed to the right and to the left of the path.

A-a-roo! A-a-roo! the wolves howled. They would tear him apart. They would shred his flesh and swallow him, bones and all. The path was clear ahead of him, cutting directly through the pack of wolves. He could see it. But now, it was not so clear behind him. If he went back, he might lose his way. What was the true thing to do? He started to scramble along a side detour, terror pushing him with its eager hand. He lost his footing in the ash heap and twisted his knee. He gripped frantically at a protruding bar of iron in the rubbish, slowing his slide. Wait. Wait. What was the truth here? What was the truth? The Rule. The Rule. "One: Do not take any detours or shortcuts."

Little Child took the silver-handled workman's hatchet from his survival kit. Holding it before him, he slowly . . . slowly . . . began to inch his way back to the path. The detours were a sore temptation, but taking them he might lose his way. Five steps forward, a slipping down. Forward despite his throbbing knee, a sliding again. Forward against his fear pushing him back. He crested the hill for the second time. At the sight of him, the wolves below bayed frantically, *A-a-roo! A-a-roo! Yap! Yap! Yap!*

Little Child began to slide stiff-legged down the hill. Beads of sweat glistened on his forehead. The handle of the hatchet felt slick in his palm. Looking behind, he watched small avalanches of falling garbage bury the path; the way to retreat had now completely disappeared. Inching, sliding, he reluctantly went forward. Closer . . . closer . . . Now a yellow light of hunger showed in the eyes of the yapping wolves. Their lips curled. Their teeth were bared. Froth foamed at their jaws.

"To the King," he spoke aloud, and the words seemed to come from somewhere inside him. "To the Kingdom." Strength filled his arm. A surge of power firmed his grip. "Though I am traveling alone, I am not really alone," he repeated to himself. "Rule Two." And at this moment he remembered he was in the hearts of all who loved him.

Suddenly he wanted battle, he wanted to howl back as loudly as the wolves: *A-a-rooo! A-a-rooo!* Nothing would stop him from serving alongside his older brother. How dare anyone try?! Others had made Crossing alone before him. He too would do brave acts for the King. Lifting his head in the direction of the Bright City, he yelled forth the mighty challenge, "TO THE KINGDOM! TO THE KING! TO THE RESTORATION!"

Enraged at the thought that this motley pack of flea-bitten dogs would try to keep him from the work of the Restoration, Little Child charged, scrambling down the hill. Attacking boldly, the boy rushed the middle of the yapping pack. He planted his feet firmly, and with anger began to circle faster and faster with the hatchet before him hacking and whacking all in its way. Turn, turn; the beasts yipped. Turn, turn; they whined. As at a signal, they scrambled to flee, their tails tucked between their legs. *Yip! Yip! Yip-yip-yip-yip-yip-yip-yip!*

Little Child watched them go, amazed at their cowardly retreat. Yes! He lifted his arms and circled in victory, his fists clenched above his head. Yes!— He two-stepped a warrior's stamp on the ground. Yes! He beat on his chest. Yes! He was a mighty warrior: Little Child, the Solitary Victor in the Battle of the Wolves. Mercie always said, "The fear is more in the going than in the doing." Yes!

But before he had a moment to savor his victory, a choking darkness descended, an ominous fog that blinded his vision. He could no longer see the path before him. Was it night so soon? Had the Battle of the

Wolves taken the afternoon? The drumbeat he had been hearing all through Crossing quickened. *Din. Din. Din. Din.*

And he remembered a scene from long ago, from a time before he knew Great Park, when he truly was a little child. *Two boys fleeing from Enchanted City . . . oo-mb-pha . . . oo-mb-pha. The deathdrums pursuing . . . oo-mb-pha . . . oo-mb-pha . . . oo-mb-pha-din.*

Confusing shadows, gray and ominous, lurched at him, bumped him. Fear battered, trapping his breath in his chest. He choked on the stink in the air. His twisted knee hobbled him. He fought for firm footing. Had nightlife caught him between Great Park and the Bright City? Was he now under the Enchanter's power? Leering yellow eyes peered out of the dark. Here. There. Something caught at his jacket—held. He jerked free.

Voices whispered close, whispered dread, "Nay. Nay. Nay. Too late. Too long. You are ours. Day is gone." The sound of the Naysayers' chorus stabbed a cold streak of terror between Little Child's shoulder blades. "Nay. Nay. Nay. Ours. Ours. Ours."

Wait—wait a moment. Think. Think. "Rule Three: Use your greatest gift when Crossing." What was his greatest gift? Mercie always said he had the gift of truth. Truth. So what was the truth of the matter here? The truth was: The sun was mid-high when he mounted the hill. The truth was: The battle could only have taken a few moments.

Little Child opened his survival kit. The doom drums sounded closer, sounded faster: *Oo-mb-pha. Oo-mb-pha. Din. Din. Din. Din.* He felt for the loaf of bread, broke off a morsel and ate it for strength, drank some water from the jug. He breathed deeply. Slightly calmer, he grasped the silver handle of the hatchet tightly. Not to doubt. Not to doubt. This way? That way? Where was the path? Was he still on it? Which direction was Bright City? "Rule Four: The path will always show itself to you if you wait."

He held the cool blade of the hatchet to his brow and bent his head to think. He closed his eyes. What exactly was the truth here? The truth was that he had won the Battle of the Wolves. They had fled before him. The truth was that it couldn't be night already. *Wait,* he said to himself. *Just wait a little.*

A silence descended, more terrible than the night and the noises. And then a voice, cold, ill: *You are mine. You are all mine.* The Enchanter.

Little Child lifted his head from the blade. His hand trembled. What was the truth here? Did he belong to the Enchanter? No. No. Mercie and Caretaker had called him their own. He would not doubt. "I am a King's man!" he shouted.

A shriek of terror tore the dark and the silence and the stench: *Ee-yi-yi-yi-yi-yi-yi-yi! You are mine! All mine!*

Little Child's knees buckled. He held the hatchet above his head and shouted back, "You lie! I am a King's man, and I keep the Kingsways!"

And the voice answered back: Mine. Mine. Mine. But it seemed weaker, fading, farther away.

"King's man!" *Who said that?* he wondered. These were new voices.

"Come, King's man. You are almost here!"

The darkness shifted. Wait! What was that? Something shining in—no, no; something shining *beyond* the false night. Something ahead of him? It looked like—it looked like—the shape of a city high above. Despite his fear of the dark things so near, despite his terror of the evil voice that sought to possess him, Little Child called out, "Bright City! Bright City!"

And with each shout, the choking fog of ill faded. With each shout light became brighter. Above, the sun was at early afterhigh. Little Child could see the path clearly before him. Glancing neither right nor left, he followed, not stopping to rest or to think.

"Hurrah! Hurrah!" A clamor. Then solo voices. "L.C.! Over here!"

"You made it, King's man!"

"You made Crossing alone!"

The boy lifted his eyes. There! The Bright City, dazzling in daylife. A watch-horn blared, *Croieee! Croieee!* Voices shouted: "Crossing! Crossing!"

And on the city walls and at its opened gates, a crowd of Restoration workers waved streamers and yelled, jumping up and down in welcome. And there! There among them stood a young man, tall and broad shouldered, his blue dress uniform braided with silver and light flashing off the insignia on his shoulder. Hero, his brother.

Hero loped down the path to gather Little Child into his strong embrace. "Ah, lad. I'm proud of you. I'm very proud of you. You made it alone. Was it a particularly difficult Crossing?"

"Oh, more difficult than many," answered the boy, tempted to boast with safety at hand. Then truth reminded him—"But not as hard as some, I suppose." After all, he was standing among the most seasoned fighters for the Resistance, men and women who really knew the meaning of battle.

The two brothers, one tall and muscular, the other slender and limping slightly, walked together to the gates of the city. Hero flung his arm around the boy's shoulder. "Welcome. Welcome. You made Crossing Alone and now are worthy to work in the Restoration. And how we need you, truth-teller. How we need you."

They faced each other before entering the watchgates. They clasped wrists in the Ranger clasp. The Watch cried out the old familiar shout, "The Kingdom comes!" This cry of greeting echoed from post to post, along the Ranger Surround which circled the wall of the Bright City. "The Kingdom comes!"

"The Kingdom comes!"

"The Kingdom—"

And never was there a little child more glad to receive a hero's welcome or to come at last to the safe place where the end of the crossing is also the beginning of the rest of the way.

safe places

The children in the Song Studio were learning an old folk chant. Hero and Little Child stood against the walls and listened to their practice.

"Ta-da-ta-da-ta-da-da-da," they chanted, then sang the refrain together.

In the Kingdom of light
The day shines bright!
Ta-da-ta-da-ta-da-da-da.

The Music Maestro called out, "Have you ever heard of a kingdom where outcasts were welcomed?"

A chorus shouted back, "No-o-o-o-o! Ta-da-da-dum!"

Little Child noticed that, as in every group of singers, one boy's voice cracked high above the rest.

"Have you ever heard of a kingdom where every lost child had a home?"

This time there was jostling between the children as each strove to outdo the others' enthusiasm. "NO-O-O-O-O! TA-DUM-DUM-DUM!" Then another refrain all together again:

In the Kingdom of light
Everything's all right!
Ta-da-ta-da-ta-DA-DA-DUM!

Hero motioned for Little Child to step outside. The older brother was taking the younger on a tour of Bright City. "We'll see most of the Safe Places today," he had explained. "In the old Enchanted City, children were always unsafe. First thing after New Day Rising, our Restoration workers decided to make Bright City secure for the children to play and grow and be happy and to find the King.

"In Bright City, we still have orphans who need names and families and birthdays. Children still suffer the memory of Branding. And there is still danger from the dark things who try to kidnap Lost Children and carry them away to the Garbage Dump. But at least for now in Bright City, the children who belong to the King are safe and secure—if they live by Kingsways."

Little Child had learned this morning that Safe Places were shelters of protection all through Bright City where anyone could learn the ways of the King and the Kingdom. They were places where apprentices could practice with Master Teachers and become valuable workers in the Restoration.

In Song Studio No. 5, for instance, children learned how to sing and play and compose music. Earlier the brothers had stopped by a Dance Company, where a troupe was going through stretching-out exercises to practice for the next Great Celebration. In an Artist Colony they had watched children, blissfully messy, learning to fingerprint and draw and sculpt papier-mâché. In a Cooking Corner, they saw children baking pastries and stirring in cookpots and measuring and chopping, all busily making food for the many in Bright City who still were hungry.

Although he had been very small when he and Hero fled the Enchanter and Branding and a pursuing hoard of Burners and Breakers, Little Child remembered enough of Enchanted City to see the great differences now. No longer did the people work by night and sleep by day. No longer did the city run on manmade power, which always failed right in the middle of the ninth inning. No longer did the deathdrums pound out orphan hunts. No longer did an oppressive fear clutch at the heart, or the din of the Naysayers weigh down the soul with impossibilities.

Instead, construction and restoration were going on everywhere. Soon they would reach even the poor in the ramshackle tenements of Moire Oxan. Instead, players mimed on park benches, taxis honked like trumpets in a marching band. Murals were being painted on empty, dark walls.

And fire—fire was no longer used to threaten or to brand, but to warm cold hands and feet and to make energy or light the way. Over all the sun shone, and if there was rain, you knew the sun would come again the next day or the next.

Little Child noticed, however, that soot still blackened most buildings, and many of the potholes in the streets had not been filled. Every now and then, faded graffiti on fences still declared, SEEING IS BELIEVING.

"It's very easy—" Hero was saying as he waved down a jaunty yellow taxi. Little Child noticed the new name lettered on its door, "MERCY STREET TAXI CORPS."

"Hey, Bub!" said the cabby, "Where'ja two wanna go?"

The brothers climbed into the back seat. "City Drama Center," answered Hero. "Any saboteur activity today?"

The cabby yanked a flag on the meter-reader, turned the crank to connect to streetline power, and pulled smoothly away from the curb. "Yep. Got some trouble. Power's been off and on all mornin'. Stop and start. Stop and start. But Taxi Corps is ready for 'em if 'ee start anything. Everything's oiled and in top-top shape."

Hero frowned, his face full of concern, then leaned back and reached for a small carton that was tucked into the corner of the seat beside him. "Hungry, L.C.? It's been a busy morning." Beneath a bandanna napkin, rounds of wheat crackers waited. There were also boiled eggs with their shells brightly tinted, green pears, and small jars of chilled apple juice—treats for busy passengers. Little Child chose several crackers to munch on.

"As I was saying, it's very easy to take all this for granted and to think there's no danger—" Hero interrupted himself, "Oh, look! Over there—you probably don't remember—used to be the Dagoda, the Enchanter's headquarters. Now it's the Mercantile Exchange, a place for buying and selling. The fruit and vegetable displays themselves are worth a visit."

Little Child peered through the taxi window at the tall building, which a crew of workmen were busy repainting. He noticed bright new banners waving from the towers. He tried to catch snatches of the hearty worksong that wafted through the air.

Hero took a swallow of the juice and leaned back. "But we need to be careful, because there still is much danger in Bright City. It's not safe like Great Park. Though the Enchanter and his host have been vanquished to the Garbage Dump, and though we live daylives, the dark things will do whatever they can to breach the Ranger Surround of protection. We are really a city under attack."

The engine of the taxi sputtered. The cab jerked to a halt, then lurched forward as the cabby ground the crank firmly and gunned the ignition. The cab lurched again, stopped, and started. "See what I mean?" the cabby said, looking over his shoulder.

Hero leaned forward, tapped the cabby and said, "That's not good. Stop here anyway. We'll cut across to the Drama Center, and I'll be there if you need me."

Switching to cell storage, the cabby left them curbside, ignited the engine, picked up speed, then—*HARNK! HARNK!*—it hustled into traffic and disappeared around the corner of a busy intersection.

Hero's face still showed concern. "We'll walk through this Play Plaza. You know, of course, that the Enchanter hates it when children play. He only wants them to work for him. He despises lighthearted laughter.

If he could, he would rob all children of their happy childhoods. All who worked for him in Enchanted City grew up too soon or didn't grow up at all. His dragnets captured orphans and trapped Lost Children. He branded five year olds at Burning Place. And he forbade birthday parties."

The two walked through a high gate between stone walls where gardeners were busy planting. "This is the first Play Plaza to be planted," Hero explained. Tall trees and shrubs sat crowded beside each other, their roots wrapped in burlap balls. A team of mothers, grandfathers, and gardeners knelt on their knees digging flowers into rich black soil. Everyone seemed to recognize Hero and to call out welcome to him.

"We'll cut catty-corner over to the walkway along the river. That way you can at least get a glimpse of the Solar Fields. Does it look at all familiar in here?"

Little Child had noticed the resemblances in the Play Plaza right away. The gates and the stonework of the outside fence were an exact copy of the one in Great Park. He supposed the trees and the flowering plants had been transported from there across the Garbage Dump.

Some children were bouncing on pogo balls in the middle of stacks of flat stones to be used for paving. Hero explained, "Caretaker has designed some twenty of these plazas all across Bright City. The idea is to transplant a little of Great Park here. These are Safe Places too."

The brothers passed through the Play Plaza out an opposite gate. A brass plaque on the stonewall displayed the engraved words, "Great Park II." Hero led Little Child across a cobblestone path to a retaining fence that overlooked a river. He lifted one foot to the bottom bar and leaned over the top. "Greenstream—except it isn't yet." A dark murky ribbon, little more than a sludge dump, poked along beneath them. He smiled at Little Child, "But one day . . . one day the Restoration will reach it. And then it really will be Greenstream."

Hero pointed to the hills beyond. "See that silver flash in the sunlight—that's where the Solar Fields are being built. Then behind the mountain is the Power Project. It's there that we've been having trouble with power-outs. The engineering team can't locate what's wrong. And this could be dangerous for Bright City."

A peal of carillon bells sounded in the air. Little Child looked questioningly at Hero, who explained, "Midday high chimes. If we hurry, maybe we'll be in time for a little of the practice at the Drama Center."

The two started to pace in stride, and although the older brother slowed his steps so the younger could stay beside, Little Child was soon breathless trying to keep up. "WHA-hat I want to KN-know is how the EN-chanter gets past the RA-ranger surround."

Hero furrowed his brow but kept jogging. "Well, sadly, many people have lived in the night so long, they don't really believe in the King. They still live under the Enchanter's rule: SEEING IS BELIEVING. And the orphans' hearts are filled with fear. You know that sighting the King is like playing a neverending game. We all played it often enough in Great Park. Well, Lost Children don't know how to play. They don't know how to sing or dance or make stories. They have to be taught. So they can't see the King, and those who don't see the King and don't believe in him often let the Enchanter's men into the Bright City."

Little Child stopped short, stunned. He thought of the horror of the old dark city. He looked around him at all the vigorous signs of Restoration. "You—you mean—they open the watchgates? Who would do such a thing?"

Hero took his arm and pulled him along. "Not exactly. Actually, we all have to be careful not to let the Enchanter's dark things breach the Protection."

"HOW-how? BUT-but HOW-how?" Little Child's question jogged as he started running again.

"This is very important for you to remember, so listen well. The Rules for Protection are as needful as the Rules for Crossing. First, whenever you live as a One Only, you are in danger. Whenever the hum of the hatchet becomes foolishness, you are in danger. When you forget to keep watch for the King, you are in danger. When you begin to keep secrets from your closest friends, when you find that you love darkness more than light, then you are in great danger. Understand?"

Little Child nodded his head as he jogged.

"If any of us are not careful—if we break the Rules for Protection—the Burners and the Breakers and the Naysayers are given power. And when they have power, they will use it to breach the Surround. Make sure you memorize the Rules."

The brothers had reached the Drama Center. They vaulted up a series of steps and went through a crescent of open doors into a large enclosed pavilion that gave way to an amphitheater lined by three tiers of balconies. A group of players stood on the stage, huddled together in conference.

"Thespia!" called Hero. "Thespia! I want you to meet my brother."

A young woman stepped away from the group, her face turned to see who had called. When she spied Hero, her smile became a radiant greeting, and she lifted an arm to wave. Little Child thought she was the most beautiful young woman he had ever seen.

She hurried toward him with hand extended.

"Thespia, this is my brother, L.C."

"Oh, welcome to Bright City, L.C. I heard you made Crossing Alone. Your brother could hardly wait to see you."

Little Child clasped her hand in the Ranger way, wrist resting on wrist, the pulse beats touching and the hands grasping each other's forearm. Close up she was as beautiful as she had been from far away. She looked again at Hero. "And you," she said quietly so that Little Child standing close could hardly hear, "now you are no longer a One Only."

Little Child knew that something important had been said between them, some meaning beyond the words that he could not fathom.

"Well now," Thespia smiled gaily. "I suppose you have landed at the Drama Center at lunchtime because you know we have a great cook. Can you stay? We're just breaking from morning practice. We'll eat and then see if we've learned anything. Street Theatre this afternoon."

Little Child swiped his sweaty face with his loosened shirt tail, which he then tucked down into his pants. He smiled shyly, "M-must have been some reason we ran all the way from G-Great Park."

She smiled back at him, then at Hero. "And how is that restoration project coming?" Without waiting for his answer, Thespia pushed a strand of hair off her forehead and tightened the ribbon that held the curling cascade at the nape of her neck. She moved off stage. "Why don't you follow me? The weather is so nice, we're eating in the courtyard outside. I'll give you a quick backstage tour on the way."

The three clambered to the stage and across the floorboards into the wings. Little Child gaped at the high scaffoldings, the stacked struts. Thespia demonstrated which pulleys moved which objects and turned the house lights on full. They flickered, then brightened, then flickered. They heard running footsteps, and saw someone racing down an aisle. "Hero! Hero!"

Hero stepped to stage right. It was the MERCY STREET TAXI CORPS cabby. "Oh, good. I found ya. We got trouble out at the Power Project. Energy is failing in the pendrants. All Ranger Leaders are gathering. Think you better come fast."

Hero glanced questioningly at Thespia, who nodded. He bent to Little Child. "I'll go check this out, then I'll pick you up sometime this afternoon. You can watch the street theater." And before they could reply, Hero had vaulted off stage, down the aisles, and out the door.

The inside lights in the theatre flickered again. The floods at the floorboards dimmed. The power connection moaned and ground to a halt.

"Oh, no," groaned Thespia. "Another power-out. They've been having trouble. And no one seems to be able to fix it. If it doesn't get fixed soon, it will be dangerous for all. Come on." She smiled at Little Child. "Meanwhile, we shall eat outside in the daylight—that never fails."

The troupe, wearing scattered odds and ends of practice costumes—a wig here, pantaloons there, clown makeup—were crowded around a long table and filling their plates full. Cook teased and bossed. He waved in the air with his spoon.

Everyone welcomed Little Child and inquired about Crossing. Thespia sat down beside him, and they pushed close on the benches to make room.

Suddenly overwhelmed by all that was new, with Hero gone and Great Park and Mercie and Caretaker far away, with Bright City being both less and more than he expected, Little Child picked at his food. He felt a warm gentle pressure on his spine, between his shoulder blades. Thespia's hand rested there, her head was turned down toward him, her strawberry-blonde hair tumbled over her far shoulder. The soft light in her eyes was shining as she studied him. Quietly, she whispered, as if to remind him, as if she knew what he was feeling, "To the King . . ."

And he answered, "To the Restoration . . ." He wanted to ask her more about power-outs. He wanted to ask her how much danger Bright City was in.

"Th-Thespia?"

"Yes, L.C.?"

He stared down at his food, his eyes shyly downcast from her gentle gaze. Instead he asked, "What is a One Only?"

"Oh, it's someone who feels—well, probably a lot like you're feeling right now. Someone who is often lonely."

"B-but . . . but Hero said if you are a One Only you are in danger? . . ."

"Yes, if you stay a One Only for any length of time, you are."

"But wh-why is Hero a One Only? Everyone here l-loves and welcomes him. Everyone needs him and knows him. He is a R-Ranger Leader."

Thespia smiled and folded her fists beneath her chin, resting her elbows on the table. She gazed ahead of her as though thinking about the right answer. "Well, becoming a One Only can happen differently for different people. Let's just say that Hero loves someone in a way that someone can't love him." She looked back to see if he understood.

"And . . . and . . . is Hero in danger?"

Thespia stood from the table and brushed the crumbs from her skirt. She pulled Little Child from his place, smoothed his unruly hair back from his forehead the way Mercie always did. Then she placed both hands on his shoulders, one on each side, and looked him directly in the eyes. The Most Beautiful Player of All smiled again. "I think today, L.C., that Hero, your brother, is in much less danger than he has been." She tapped him on the nose. "All because you have come."

power-outs

Benji stood high on a metal catwalk overlooking hundreds of shining panels placed strategically in the Solar Field outside the city limits. He listened to the turbine motors of the new wind-catchers: *thrmmm, thrmmm, thrmmm*.

Sounds good so far. But Benji was uneasy. For some reason, the engines kept slipping. He took his clock-stop from his gray powerworker crew jacket and punched the button to time the sequences in case the turbines missed cycles. How he hoped they wouldn't slip out again. Another power-out would be terrible. How could they say that Kingsways were better than the Enchanter's if the power was always failing?

Benji was a young man, no longer the sniveling fearful brat terrified of the alarm, "Power-out! Power-out!" No longer the lonely boy dreading the gurgling in the tubes of the underwater sewer system which meant that the lights "up there" were failing, and he and Eddie and the orphans below would suffer the Enchanter's wrath.

In those days, Benji and Eddie, his best friend, were known as the Sewer Rat and the Boiler Brat. Miserable orphans, forced by the evil Enchanter to man the dark, damp, ever-failing powerworks, they had been loyal buddies. And one day, into their dank and hopeless underworld a Stranger had come, humming a fragment of a hauntingly beautiful tune and promising to teach them the whole song. So the two boys and all the other cold and hungry rats and brats had followed the man to "up there."

The man led them to Great Park, where Mercie and Caretaker loved them and sheltered them and taught them to laugh again. The boys learned all the notes to many songs. They grew strong and tall and wanted to make a difference in the world. And when the time came, first Eddie and then Benji had made the fearful Crossing back from Great Park into the City. They were eager to risk its hazards to be part of the early Restoration, and together the two had vowed before Ranger Commander: No more power-outs. No more misery in the underworld for children. No more forced firings. No more helpless victims thrown into the clogged sewage wastelines.

But somewhere along the way, something had happened to their friendship. They were no longer best buddies . . . in fact, they hardly spoke.

Now Benji the young man, powerworker for the Restoration, stood above the field of energy collectors listening nervously for a catch in the turbine motors. There had been ten power-outs since summer. Vigilantes reported Naysayers breaching the Surround at night and creeping through the neighborhoods chanting: *Nay. Nay. What New Day Rising? Nay. Nay. Nay. What King?* Neither the powerchecks nor any of the powerworkers could find any flaw in the mechanisms.

Surely these days everyone knew that Kingsways were far superior to the Enchanter's way. But still, there were those who missed living in the night—the night crawlers. And these breakdowns gave power to the dark things. Saboteurs breached the Surround and hid in the shadows of the city. Power-outs reminded people of the old ways and made them afraid.

Thr/—mm. Thr/—mm. He did not like the way the hum in the turbines halted. Benji leaned on the metal railing and watched the clockstop in his hand tick off seconds and minutes. Something was wrong. Benji checked the clockstop time. He wrote it down on a chartboard. The wind-catcher turbines began choking and sputtering. Grinding and moaning, the machinery complained: *Thr/Thr/Thr.* The flashing blades which had been speeding round and round slowed, then stopped. *Thr-thr-thr-thr-thr. Thrank.*

Aw-w-w-w-w-w, now what? An alarm started to ring: *Aooga! Aooga! Aooga!* The speakerloud announced: "Attention. All Section Managers. Power-out! Attention. All Section Managers. Power-out!"

Benji hated the thought of facing Ranger Commander with another power failure. He slid down the tower pole rather than waste time on the stairs and met other powerworkers rushing to the Command Center. *Aooga! Aooga! Aooga!*

The tall Ranger Commander was standing in the middle of the theater where a strategy panel with a flat surface could be surveyed by all those gathered. Ranger squad leaders had hurried to the emergency session. Commander pointed with a long marker, "This pendrant and this pendrant are now without energy. The Mercantile Exchange is energy-futile and the Healing House also."

Everyone in the room groaned. The exchange would take a dip, causing hardship on the merchants. Shoppers would not be able to buy food. Milk would spoil. Sick people would have to be evacuated to Safe Places, causing them to have setbacks in their healthlines.

Ranger Commander assigned duties to Ranger Leaders, who immediately rushed off to waiting taxis that would hasten them to the energy-futile pendrants. There they would command local strategy and vigilantes to ward off enemy infiltration.

Ranger Commander's eyes were stern. "I believe we have finally isolated our difficulty. It seems there has been a minor but devastating miscalculation between upslope and downslope speeds. Immediate steps will be taken to correct the damage. And certain powerworkers will be assigned to eliminate the miscalculation. Powerworker Eddie. Powerworker Benji. Please report. The rest of Power Project crew, to your posts. Dismissed."

Everyone departed quickly, relieved that some miscalculation had finally been isolated. For the first time since summer, Eddie and Benji were alone in the same room. Benji fleetingly wondered, for the thousandth time, what had happened to their friendship.

They walked to the middle of the circular Command Center. Ranger Commander looked at them a long time without saying a word. The silence gave much opportunity for thought. Then he spoke, his voice low and serious. "If there is a miscalculation in the upscale wind velocity and in the downscale wind velocity, then the giant blades of the wind-catchers will be tilted inaccurately. Is that correct?"

Yes, nodded the two powerworkers, looking the Commander straight in the eye.

"Go, you two," the imposing leader ordered. "Gather your records and be back here in an hour's half-time. I want to see your calculations. We are going to get to the bottom of this today."

Benji and Eddie saluted, then hastened to their work stations in their separate sections. Why had Ranger Commander singled them out? thought Benji, hurrying up the stairs and down a hallway. Was Eddie a saboteur? Or, worse, was he, Benji, the one under suspicion?

The two had gone through so much together. Soon after New Day Rising, as engineer apprentices, they had learned powercraft under the very pioneer team who had designed and built these vast acres of solar collectors. The hundreds of panels now collecting sun, gathering warmth from the air, were a testimony to the team's dedicated efforts.

Benji rounded a corner so quickly that he bumped into a maintenance man.

"Whoa!" The janitor's push broom clattered to the floor, and the mop bucket overturned, spilling sudsy water.

"Sorry!" said Benji, backing down the hall. "Sorry. Another power-out. Gotta get stuff for Ranger Commander."

"I know," said the maintenance man with a smile.

Benji was in such a hurry he didn't notice the twinkle in the man's eye.

"The problem's as plain as the nose on your face. Check out your friend."

Benji stopped to pick up the mop, but the man waved him on his way. He was down the hall before he paused and called back, "Hey! What did you say?"

The man was righting his bucket and starting to mop up the mess. "I said that the problem's right under your nose."

Not understanding, Benji hurried on to his workspace and hastily began gathering his notes. He held the stack of files, ledgers, and sheets in his arms, his mind racing. What did he mean, *The problem's right under your nose?* Benji didn't remember having seen that janitor around the Power Project before. *Check out your friend.* Was Eddie the problem right under his nose?

Perhaps the break in their friendship was unavoidable. Even in the waste water underworld, Eddie had always been more courageous. When the drains backed up, it was he who had volunteered to save the others from firing by facing popping. It was Eddie who had first seen the Stranger and believed that he could lead the rats and brats to "up there." It was Eddie who refused to escape until the others had heard the sound of the song and seen the man's soft light. How could he, Benji, ever expect to be friends for life with someone like Eddie?

Since one evening last summer, they had scarcely talked. Oh, there had been no quarrel, no angry words. There had been no pushing, no disagreement. He supposed the incident was only a sign of how far apart they had grown.

It had been an exhausting day doing energy audits on the crumbling housing in Moire Oxan. Eddie and Benji decided they deserved a sweet-treat, and checked out a Power Project repair van to drive to the Emporium for ices. Driving back, Eddie looked out the van window and saw a sliver of moon rising on the eastern horizon, cupped there for a moment in the blue-gray day's end. The other side, the western sky, was blazoned with gold-shot fuchsia rays, as the sun eased itself lazily behind the tip of the earth's edge. Clouds, suffused with color and rimmed in shadow, anticipated night.

"Oh, look!" cried Eddie. "Day and night both! Oh, Benji, look!"

Benji, at the wheel, was carefully steering with one hand and licking his ice in the other, and trying to watch the street ahead of him. He looked up at the windshield only to see an ugly, fat summer squask-bug splatter against the glass. "Aughh!" he said. "Gross! Do you want the rest of my ice?"

Eddie had given Benji the strangest look and said nothing.

It had been a little thing—that summer incident. But the two friends had hardly spoken three words to each other since. They still smiled politely and said good day and nodded their heads in greeting, but Eddie had requested reassignment to another section, saying he was tired of measuring shadow angles. He asked to be allowed to study skyscapes in order to determine the slant requirements for heat reflection. They no longer attended street theater together. They no longer harmonized the songs of Great Celebration.

Benji checked his timepiece. He was due back in the Powerworks Command Center in ten minutes. He sat at his desk for a moment and recalled the differences that had existed between himself and Eddie even as boys. As Sewer Rat No. 1, Eddie had longed for "up there." In Great Park, the clouds and the vast spaces were amazing to him. And here in Bright City, it seemed to him that the old unwelcome cry, "Power-out! Power-out!" would never again be necessary if someone could only learn to harness the energy of the wind. Eddie loved to study the way birds soared in flight. He wondered about the universe. He could never quite believe he was really "up there," and he never took it for granted.

Formerly, as Boiler Brat, Benji had needed to look down. His job was to boss the crews of children who shoveled sludge into the furnaces that fired the boilers in the underworld. So, in Great Park, it was only natural that he liked to dig dirt in Mercie's garden at planting time. He liked kicking stones down the paths of Wildflower Woods, and sometimes he found things—old buttons and dropped copper coins. What if someone lost a demi-dollar and he missed it because he hadn't been looking down? That thought made him look down all the more.

And while Benji was looking down, Eddie was looking up. So things just happened between them. "Oh, Benji," Eddie would cry. "Look up! A swallowtail!"

And Benji would look up, but he never saw the swallowtails. He would invariably trip on a Great Park signpost, fall to his knees, tear his jeans, and generally feel like a klutz. Benji began to suspect that it was dangerous to look up. When you were looking up, you couldn't see where you were going. Because Benji liked to see where he was going, he looked at the ground even more and carefully plotted each step.

It was while looking down that Benji had become intrigued by shadows. The same tree could cast a long or a short shadow, depending on the time of day. He sat in Deepest Forest where everywhere was mostly shadow and watched sunlight dapple the tree trunks and the fern-covered floor.

In Bright City the boys' differences gave them each a place. Eddie, gifted in looking up, specialized in observing world climate systems. He measured sun height angles. He clocked windspeed on the upslope hills. Benji, gifted in looking down, marked shadow angles and plotted castlines. He clocked windspeed on the downslope hills.

The Power Project crew learned to depend on Eddie because he could view things far away that the rest of them had trouble seeing. The Power Project crew trusted Benji because he was so sensible. If he didn't know the answer, he knew where to find it.

So the friends had gone their separate ways. The graphs for measuring shadow angles consumed Benji's time and overflowed the files in his workplace. He was laying the schemes for efficient suncatching. With his nose glued to his charts, he figured insulation regulations. It was exacting work, tedious even, but it suited him. Nevertheless, Benji often missed the exciting companionship of his friend who was always crying, "Look up! Oh, look up!"

Time to go. Benji dreaded facing Ranger Commander. He dreaded the thought that Eddie might have fallen away from Kingsways or that he, himself, might be suspected of sabotage. How could this have happened? How could good friends drift apart?

With reluctant feet, he dragged himself to the confrontation. Benji glanced at Eddie, who was already there and waiting. Maybe Eddie thought he was a saboteur.

"I hear," said Ranger Commander, "that you two are no longer working together."

Eddie and Benji looked at each other. They looked at the ground. They nodded their heads. Commander was right. They were no longer working together; in fact, they were no longer speaking to each other.

Ranger Commander, as he was apt to do, waited a long time before speaking again. "That is correct. You have not been working together. Something has come between you. Now, answer me this question. If there is a breach in friendship, and friends miscalculate one another, could that possibly affect the Power Project?"

The silence grew. The silence in the hall was even heavier than the silence of the turbines in the valley between the hills outside. Both Eddie and Benji were remembering all the times when, working together, they had checked each other's calculations, comparing notes to make sure their estimates matched. But since summer they had avoided one another. And since summer there had been ten—now eleven—power-outs, all of which had at the least inconvenienced the people of Bright City and at the worst had harmed some.

Oh, no, they both thought at the same time. *We are the reason there are power-outs. We have failed to be faithful to our assignments.*

In surprise, Benji remembered the words of the maintenance man: *The problem is as plain as the nose on your face.* He was right! Who was that maintenance man?

Benji looked at Ranger Commander, and then he looked at Eddie. At that very moment, Eddie cried, "Man, I've missed you, Benj! You help keep my head out of the clouds! Forgive me for resenting the way you only see the things right under your nose."

Benji understood, "This is awful. We two are the problem. Missed me? I've missed you. You always keep me from dragging my feet. You make me look up."

Ranger Commander was still not smiling. His arms were folded across his chest. "Well, you two. It appears as though the whole of Bright City has missed you both. Fix the miscalculations first. Go over those upscale and downscale wind calculations until you get them right. Correct that windblade tilt. No more power-outs. Then, work on your friendship until you get it right. And that's not a suggestion. Believe me, it's a command."

With that, Ranger Commander swept from the Command Center, and the two powerworkers faced one another. They grasped hands in the Ranger clasp. Then, they spread their files on the floor and pored over their graphs and figures. They recalculated and checked one another's math, working through the night. The next morning, exhausted but relieved, they finally had discovered their miscalculations. By midday high, they and the whole Power Project heard again the satisfying *thrm-mm, thrmmm, thrmmm* of the turbines in regular cycle.

Power was restored to Bright City.

"We need a reward. Let's sign out a van and go to the Emporium for a sweettreat," Eddie said.

But when they arrived, they discovered that the ices had melted due to the power-out.

Benji laughed. "We'll have to settle for taffy-chews. But on the bright side, there won't be any squask-bugs either. Their season is past!"

Each day, Eddie and Benji reminded themselves of their vows: "No more power-outs! No more misery for orphan children! No more helpless victims! Power to Bright City!"

And they would not soon forget. For the maintenance man had taped a new poster in the hall reading, "Keep Kingsways!" And somehow they knew that was the most powerful reminder of all.

Mudslinging

Mudslinging!" The report came crackling over Central Radio Dispatch at MERCY ST. TAXI CORPS. "Mudslinging! Play Plaza No. 5."

Hero, Little Child, and Amanda were touring the taxi headquarters. Since New Day Rising and the ousting of the Enchanter, there was no need for an underground resistance. Now the taxi company was involved in rescue operations that could be carried out in broad daylight. The efficient restored garage was a command center for the Restoration.

The report came crackling again. "Mudslinging! Play Plaza No. 5. Mudslinging! Play Plaza No. 9."

Hero groaned and hurried to the strategy planning map that was mounted high and filled one whole wall. Climbing the platform, he located the two trouble spots. In frustration, he slapped his hand against the map. "Chaos," he mumbled. "Always happens after power-outs." He motioned to Amanda and Little Child to join him on the scaffolding.

The Chief Cabby hastened to the map wall and looked up, "Pendrant three and pendrant four. Whaddaya expect?"

"These were the pendrants that were energy futile in the power-out," Hero explained.

The Chief pulled an alarm bar, sounding a loud signal: *Trouble! To the streets! Trouble! To the streets!*

Hero stepped down from the platform and grasped his brother's shoulder. "This is one of the reasons power-outs are dangerous to the city, L.C. When the energy fails, some people act as though the Enchanter still ruled. They panic. They forget Kingsways. All the unplanted plazas have been scenes for recent mudslinging. For some reason, people start calling one another names and throwing dirt."

By this time the garage was rumbling with the sound of doors slamming, ignitions firing, cabbies shouting, tires squealing.

Hero shouted at Amanda, "Take L.C. with you and go in the first taxi vanguard to Play Plaza No. 5. I'll try to catch Ranger Commander. He was afraid this might happen again."

"And you"—he pointed at Little Child as he backed away—"stay in the taxi. Whatever happens, don't get out into the streets. I'm warning you, you're liable to get mud right in the face." With that, Hero and the Chief Cabby rushed away to jump into a command taxi. Its siren wailed and its flashing light began to rotate.

"Over here!" shouted a cabby to Amanda and Little Child. "Get a move on."

In short order, the yellow taxis were out onto the streets, each driver knowing exactly his or her place in the taxi vanguard and each understanding his or her responsibility.

Little Child sat tense in the back seat, watching out the windows for trouble. "Amanda? Why do the people throw mud?" This never happened in Great Park. People weren't cruel to one another there. How could this be the King's city if the people threw dirt at one another?

Amanda leaned from the front seat where she was riding watchpoint beside the driver. "City ways, I guess. Something about the power going out. I'm not sure why. But I do know we'd better get all those play plazas landscaped and planted soon."

One by one the yellow taxis rounded a corner, dispersing into a large circle with the intent of moving slowly into and through the disorder. Little Child was startled to see a mob of people gathering on opposing sides of a street outside an unfinished play plaza. Inside the stone walls, mounds of earth, readied for trees and shrubs, were piled along the walkways. Clods of dirt flew though the air. Crude signs had been hastily lettered and bobbed over the heads of the people. POWERWORKERS ARE SABOTEURS! THE CITY THAT DOESN'T WORK! People raised their fists and shouted angrily at each other.

"It's your fault!" A fistful of mud flew through the air. *Whap!*

"No. It's your fault! Power was better in the old days." More fistfuls of mud winged back across the street. *Whap! Whap!*

People pushed each other and shoved, ducked, and jostled to be in the best slinging position. Little Child was amazed to see mothers shouting from the curbs, their children beside them. They screamed and slung mud while their boys and girls watched wide-eyed. Anger pulsed through the crowd, charged with catcalls and baiting.

"Wait here," said Amanda as she opened the cab door. A roar of noise rushed in. She ducked a flying clod.

"Bu-but it's dangerous out there," Little Child replied.

"Yes!" she shouted. "That's why I said to stay in the taxi!"

The door slammed and Little Child watched as Amanda began to edge through the crowd. He could barely hear her cries, "These are not Kingsways! No name-calling! No mudslinging!" She was swallowed up in the angry jostling.

His heart pounding, Little Child settled anxiously into the seat. The cabby monitored dispatches over his radio, signaling his position, then at a command—"Taxis advance!"—drove slowly, slowly, parting the shouting crowd. The boy pressed his nose against the back window. A glob of mud hit the glass. *Smack!*

He jerked his face back in surprise. Had someone flung dirt at him? The messy clod slid to the ground, and then a stooping form came running past, scooped up the mud, took aim and whanged it back into the crowd. "Hah! Gotcha!"

This was awful. How did rioting get stopped once it had started? Another mudball hit the glass and splattered across the window. *Smack!*

Little Child was suddenly enraged. He wasn't doing anything wrong. Why were they throwing the mud at him? He wanted to open his door, scoop up the dirt and toss it himself. And where was Amanda?

Meanwhile the cabby kept inching the taxi deeper, deeper into the fracas. It was from this position that Little Child could clearly see the opposing mobs, each on one side of the street. "Ya want dirt? You'll get dirt!" *Splat! Splat!*

And wha-a-a? Who was that? Who was that man in the middle of the street, that streetcleaner with a cart and push brooms and shovels and a dustbin? What an odd and dangerous thing to be doing, cleaning the mud right in the middle of the fight. And how useless! The more he shoveled, the more mud landed in the street.

The people screamed back and forth, "We know Kingsways better than you know Kingsways!" *Whap!*

"No! We sight the King more than you sight the King!" *Whap!*

In the middle of all this, Little Child could see that the man was wearing workingman's dungarees, a flannel shirt, a hardhat, and steel-toed boots. As the boy watched, the streetcleaner said nothing. He scarcely glanced about him, but just kept cleaning and sweeping and shoveling the mess.

A fistful of mud hit the man in the chest. He neither shouted in anger or threw the dirt back at the crowd; he didn't even wipe the clinging filth from his shirt.

A little girl, yelling "Nah-ah-ah-ah-ah!" as loudly as the adults beside her, got pushed from the curb, took a direct hit in the face, and started to howl, but the crowd was screaming so stridently they couldn't hear her.

The streetcleaner walked to her, and with mud flying all around him, took her in his arms, pulled a clean handkerchief from his pocket, and wiped the filth from her face. No word escaped his lips, but his searching eyes found the little girl's mother, who took her daughter, looked at the man for one long moment, and shamefacedly slipped out of the crowd and disappeared.

Who was that man? Little Child wondered to himself. The boy couldn't see his face because it was hidden by the brim of the hardhat and the jostling commotion, but something seemed vaguely familiar about him.

By now the taxi vanguard had circled the entire Play Plaza and the crowd on opposing sides. At a signal, the cab horns began to beep. *Harnk! Harnk! Harnk!* Soon the furious voices of the people were smothered in the chorus of taxi horns. *Harnk! Harnk! Harnk!* Somewhere nearby, Little Child thought other voices were now echoing Amanda's cries, "People! People of Bright City! These are not Kingsways! These are not the ways of the King!"

With its siren wailing and its lights flashing, a command taxi pulled into the center of the street. Boldly Ranger Commander emerged, tall and handsome, his dark, gray-streaked head above those of most people in the crowd. His eyes were stern, flashing displeasure. He raised his hands above his head, palms open and out in an appeal for reason. Then he turned round, facing the other side of the street. Seeing him, the people began to fall quiet. They ditched the mud from their hands. Their placards suddenly fell to the ground and were trampled under foot in the hopes that no one would remember they had just jutted and bobbed above the angry scene.

The radio dispatch crackled, "Play Plaza No. 9 is in riot. Reposition. Reposition."

Amanda appeared, breathless, at the front door of the taxi. "Ranger Commander will soon have Play Plaza No. 5 under control. Let's see if we can help in the next pendrant."

The cabby gently beeped his horn, maneuvering the taxi backward through the crowd. The people were now standing with their shoulders hunched and their heads bent, and they yielded easily to the taxi. The strong voice of Ranger Commander could be heard through the window,

"The Kingdom is any place people do the King's work and live by the King'sways!"

Little Child searched the subdued and chastened mob to find the streetcleaner, but the man was nowhere in sight.

At Play Plaza No. 9, the same angry scene greeted them. People shouting. Signs bobbing. Mud flying. *Whap!* Again Amanda hastened from the taxi, giving the same warning to Little Child. The radio crackled with signals. Again, two opposing camps lined opposite sides of a street. Again, globs of mud hit the taxi windows.

The people shouted back and forth: "No, we're the King's people!" *Whap!*

To his amazement, Little Child saw another streetcleaner in the middle of the street. Like the first, he was pushing his broom, shoveling up tossed clumps of dirt, scooping it all into a bin in his cart and not saying a word. Wait, thought Little Child. Was this another streetcleaner, or was it the same man? It certainly looked like him. Same dungarees. Same flannel shirt. Same hardhat and boots. Could it be? How had he moved his cart through the streets to this place of conflict and arrived before the taxi?

Little Child watched the streetcleaner. He never shouted, he never threw back the clods of mud that hit him. A big man with an angry scowl stepped off the curb and shook his fist in the streetcleaner's face. The streetcleaner said nothing, but looked long and silently at the giant of a man. Suddenly the accuser thrust his threatening fist into his pocket, backed off, turned, and ran out of the mob.

Who was this streetcleaner? Little Child wondered again. And as the crowd swirled around the taxi, he forgot Amanda and Hero's warnings and opened the door to get a better look. First he stood on the fender, rocking up and down, then he boosted himself higher onto the trunk. Chants swirled around his head: "No more power-outs! No more power-outs! The old ways are just as good!"

A clod hit him in the back, but he scarcely noticed. From this height, he could clearly see the streetcleaner standing absolutely still. Mud hit the man's cheek. At the impact his hardhat tumbled to the street, and the man wiped blood from his eyes. Little Child gasped—they were putting stones in the mud! And then, then he could see the man's hair, the gold glinting in the brown. Despite the turmoil of the people, the boy caught a full glimpse of the streetcleaner's face.

At that, Little Child clambered from the taxi and pressed through the mob. "Make way. Make way." He had to get closer. Without pausing to think, he stepped into the street beside the streetcleaner. He did know this man. Little Child fell at the man's feet, tears blinding his eyes.

The streetcleaner stopped sweeping, rested his broom against the cart, and drew the boy to full stature. He looked quietly at Little Child, and his eyes were filled with the greatest sadness that Little Child had ever seen. "Ah lad," said the man. "And are you the only one standing by me to help clean up all this mudslinging?"

Little Child gulped and shook his head yes. He grabbed a push-broom and began to sweep beside the streetcleaner. At first the crowd jeered and aimed mud at the dustbin. Then, when neither the man nor the boy replied in kind, mudslingers on both sides of the street threw mud at them.

As he had in Plaza No. 5, the streetcleaner guided a lost, frightened child to its parent. And after one long look and no words, the father lifted his child out of the dreadful melee and turned toward home. The shouts and the screams began to lessen. In silence the streetcleaner held out his hand, and a few people gave him their accusing placards, which he junked in the dustbin.

Little Child worked beside the streetcleaner, and the man paused a moment to brush the mud from the boy's shoulders. In return, Little Child did the same for him. Seeing this, several people in the crowd, as though coming to their senses, turned to one another and brushed away the clods of dirt. Only a few were still shouting. Then, as though thinking the same thought at the same time, from both sides of the street several people walked to the bin and ditched their placards. Some took brooms and shovels from the cart and began to clear away the dirt.

A growing silence, a silence as still as the streetcleaner's own, descended upon the crowd. Had they really been throwing mud at one another? How in Bright City had this begun? And why had it gone on so long? How had the anger become so hot and pitched?

Little Child looked again into the eyes of the man. Yes, the boy had seen him before, joyfully playing with the children of Great Park. He had seen him riding tall on the backs of the great elk as Ranger Commander and Mercie surveyed the forest. He had seen him dancing the steps of the Great Celebration. He had seen him as the most beautiful of men, had heard his voice commanding the winds and the thunder. Little Child had seen the lights in his eyes and known his laughter rolling out over all of Deepest Forest, over Wildflower Woods, over the Practice Field and Mercie's Cottage, that laughter that made every heart feel at peace, feel that all was well after all.

It was the King, the King who had endured Burning Place to lift the dark enchantment which had held the city in the Enchanter's power. Little Child had never seen him as now, in disguise like a common streetsweeper, his hands callused from hard work, his face filthy from thrown dirt, pain shadowing his eyes. It was the King now cleaning up the mud the people of his kingdom had been slinging at one another. It was the King, suffering silently the blows of dirt that fell on him. It was the King with a wound on his cheek.

By now, the taxi vanguard had again circled the crowd. But this time there was no honking of horns. A quiet, heavy and raw, had already fallen. Standing in the middle of the street, surrounded by people who had just been slinging mud at one another and shouting hateful words, Little Child could stay silent no longer. Truth, the words of truth came pushing urgently out of his heart. "People of the city! The King! Your King! This man is the King!"

At that, the people looked at the man and with their anger finally vented, they saw him and knew him and realized what they had done. And Little Child, unable to bear the shame he felt as witness to their deeds, rushed into the streetcleaner's arms and sobbed, his nose made muddy by his tears rubbing against the dirt still on the man's dungaree bib and flannel shirt. The streetcleaner embraced him and patted his back, and whispered softly so that only the boy could hear, "Hush now. Hush. Hush. You have cleaned the streets with me. Good job, my boy. Good job."

And as Little Child wept, one by one the members of the mob quietly left Play Plaza No. 9, trampling underfoot the placards which had so crudely declared: We know the King'sways better than you!

The Girl with the Very Loud Outside Voice

Agatha Ann was a little girl with a very loud outside voice. Her mother kept saying to her, "Agatha Ann! Agatha Ann! Please use your gentle inside voice. Your outside voice is too loud for indoors."

Agatha Ann tried. She would speak her next thought

quietly. But after a while she would forget. "HEY!" she would shout when she was shopping with her mother. "CAN WE BUY SOME PRETZEL-TREATS? CAN I CARRY THE SHOPPING BASKET? ARE THERE ANY LONGBREADS FOR SUPPER?"

People covered their ears. Windows rattled. Vendors way on the other side of the Mercantile Exchange raised their eyebrows as if to say to one another, *Yup. Agatha Ann is here again. Ya' know. Da little girl wid da loud outside voice.*

Agatha Ann's mother would warn her, "Now, Agatha Ann, if you can't use a gentle inside voice, I can't take you with me to the Mercantile Exchange."

And Agatha Ann would promise. She certainly would use her gentle inside voice. Yes, she would. Please. Please take her. She would be good. She would remember.

Agatha Ann loved the Mercantile Exchange. It was a wondrous bazaar in the middle of Bright City set up in a historic structure once called the Dagoda. Here tradesmen and women unfurled their canopies over their booths. Homegrown fruits and vegetables were piled on brightly-patterned cloths. Free samples, apple slices, broken tidbits of crackers, crumbled raisin cakes were given for testing. People traded what they didn't want for what they did want.

Several wide outer aisles circled the colorful displays of inside booths. Here children whose parents were shopping could play games with their friends. They could slide on slick boards. They could hop double-scotch jumprope. They could play loop-the-loop by rolling hoops. Jugglers and sleight-of-hand masters, puppeteers and stilt-walkers kept the children entertained so that they would not become tired and cranky and test their parents' patience.

No one bought more than they needed in the Mercantile Exchange so that demand would not exceed supply. Huge bins stood at the outside entrances and exits. Here shoppers and merchants donated what was excess so that poor children would have a few nice toys, some warm and new clothes, shoes without holes in the soles, or fresh healthy food.

It was a testimony to the power of Agatha Ann's loud outside voice that it could be heard over the happy clamor in the Mercantile

Exchange. Vendors shouted, "Melons! New potatoes! Tomatoes! Rutabagas!" Shoppers and sellers bartered, "Give you this-for-that! Give you that-for-this!"

Yet the little girl's voice could be heard from one side to another, and people covered their ears when she spoke. "HEY! MOM! CAN I PLAY IN THE OUTER RING? CAN I BUY GOOD GRAIN COOKIES FOR SOME OF MY FRIENDS? CAN I HAVE A COIN TO PUT IN THE SHAREBIN?"

Agatha Ann tried to use her gentle inside voice, but she always forgot, much to her mother's embarrassment. One day while the two were shopping for lamb's wool to knit into sweaters, Agatha Ann cried, "OH, LET'S GET GREEN WOOL! I LOVE GREEN WOOL!" And five windows on the opposite side of the Exchange cracked and shattered.

It was then that members of the Mercantile Meisterboard approached Agatha Ann's mother. These were the market masters who decided which merchants should sell wares in which booths. The Meisterboard regulated prices, checked to see that the scales were honest and the registers true. It made sure that all goods were artfully displayed, that the hot food sold by vendors was not only tasty but nourishing, that happy events were planned for the many children who came shopping with their parents.

Sorry to say, the Chief Mercantilemeister explained, Agatha Ann's outside voice was just too loud for inside. Many sellers and buyers had complained about this before. The board would like to suggest a solution. When Agatha Ann came to the Exchange with her mother, if she would just wait in the Cold Storing Locker where the cuts of meats were hung and prepared, ice chips were made, and fast-freezing vats froze foods, then, they said, her very loud outside voice would not bother other shoppers, and she could use it inside as much as she liked without hurting anyone's ears.

This solution made everyone happy. The other shoppers were happy. The venders and sellers were happy. Agatha Ann's mother was happy. Whenever the two came to the Mercantile Exchange, Agatha Ann would go to the door of the Cold Storing Locker and knock. Then she would enter and sit on a cold hard bench. She would bundle herself in her coat, pull out her mittens, even in summer, and shiver. *I will learn to use my gentle inside voice all the time when I am inside. I will speak in nothing above a whisper,* she would say to herself over and over. But the next thing she knew, despite all her efforts, sitting alone in the Cold Storing Locker, she would suddenly realize she was shouting, "I WILL NEVER USE MY VERY LOUD OUTSIDE VOICE INSIDE AGAIN!"

Yes, everyone was pleased with this solution except Agatha Ann. She was not happy about it at all. She missed the busy buying and selling, the bright stripes of the canopies over the booths, the free cookies and banana-halves and fresh strawberry treats. She wanted to watch the wondrous magicians and jugglers. She wanted to drop her hard-saved pennies and her still-good outgrown clothes into the Sharebins. She wasn't a bad little girl. She just had a very loud outside voice that she couldn't remember not to use inside. But people who heard her loud voice never got to know how hard she tried to be quiet, how much she practiced speaking softly. Tears dropped to her cheeks and froze like delicate flakes of tissue.

One day as Agatha Ann was sitting on the cold hard bench practicing over and over her gentle inside voice, she heard someone ask a question, "Why, little girl, whatever are you doing here?" Agatha Ann looked up into the kind face of a woman all dressed in white. She was wearing a white fur cap, white earmuffs, a white coat, white gloves, white leggings, and soft white felt boots.

"I'M PRACTICING MY GENTLE INSIDE VOICE!" shouted Agatha Ann, not realizing she was really using her very loud outside voice inside again. A large cloud of vapor puffed out of the little girl's mouth and floated to the ceiling. "WHO ARE YOU?"

The woman smiled. "Some people call me the ice lady. Say, you make wonderful puffs of airbreaths. You must have a very loud outside voice. I can even hear you while wearing my earmuffs. I can't hear most people who speak in gentle inside voices. I have to lift my earmuffs, and then my ears get red and chapped, particularly if these people have a lot to say. I have chilblains when I go home at night after listening to them. But I can hear you just fine. It's quite nice."

Large tears swelled in Agatha Ann's eyes. They dropped down her cheeks and toward her ears, making her look as though her face was sprinkled with chipped diamonds. This was the first time anyone had ever said anything nice about her very loud outside voice. She had always thought there must be something good about being so noisy. "WHAT DO YOU DO?" the little girl asked.

The ice lady laughed because she could actually hear Agatha Ann's words. Her laugh formed a thin sheet of breath-ice, which cracked as it came out of her mouth and fell at their feet in a hundred sparkling shards. "Oh, I'm the Coldmeister. I make sure that the Cold Storing Locker works. Today it seems to be working exceptionally well." She sat beside Agatha Ann on the hard bench. "Did the Mercantile Meisterboard decide that you should come here?"

Agatha Ann sniffed her nose and nodded her head yes. The frozen tears on her cheeks glistened, flying up and down as she shook her head. "THEY SAY MY OUTSIDE VOICE IS TOO LOUD FOR INSIDE! AND I CAN'T SEEM TO LEARN TO USE A GENTLE INSIDE VOICE! THEY SAY THAT PEOPLE HAVE COMPLAINED!"

"They say, they say," the Coldmeister shook her head. "Well, we have to remember that the Marketmeisters are well-meaning folk. They have to be concerned about what is good for everyone at the Mercantile Exchange. You know, fair prices and a pleasant environment for shopping and such." The woman in white patted the little girl's mittens with her own gloved hand. "But it would have been nice if someone could have seen the wonder in having a very loud outside voice."

Agatha Ann looked up in surprise.

"Does your mother know how wonderful your outside voice is?"

The little girl sighed, hunched her shoulders and looked down, "No. She just wishes that I could learn to use my gentle inside voice."

"Well, we have to remember that mothers are also well-meaning folk. They have to be concerned about raising children who will behave properly and whom other people will like. This, we must not forget, is a very difficult task."

Together the two sat in silence, thinking about these difficult jobs. The rumble of the ice-chip machine could be heard in the Locker.

"I wonder," said the Coldmeister. "Since everything seems to be working exceptionally well today, if you might have time for me to tell you a story?" And without waiting for an answer, since it was obvious to them both that Agatha Ann had lots of time, the woman in white began.

"Once there was a little girl—about your age or maybe a little younger—who used to cry and screech at the worst of moments. At the very worst of moments." For a minute, the lady in white paused, and her eyes seemed to gaze at a faraway place in a long ago time.

"This little girl lived when the evil Enchanter ruled the City with terrible enchantments, before the good King gave himself at Burning Place to free the City from the spells. You've heard about that time, haven't you?"

Agatha Ann nodded her head.

"Well, this little girl was an orphan. She didn't have a nice mommy like you. And in the old days, before the King came out of Exile, orphans belonged to the Enchanter. And this little orphan was a Sewer Rat, part of the crews of forced child labor in the underwater system of sewer pipes and boilers. And because she was so little, she could crawl into places the bigger Rats and Brats couldn't reach. But she was always afraid. And because she was always afraid and cold and hungry, she cried a lot. And when she was really afraid, she screeched and hollered and called for her mama who was long dead. And when she screeched, the Enchanter's evil workers made her walk barefoot over hot coals. This was called firing. You've heard about firing, haven't you?"

Yes. Yes, Agatha Ann had. She sat on the bench quietly, her eyes very wide and her own tears forgotten. "Wha-what happened to the little girl?" Without even trying, Agatha Ann had spoken in a gentle inside voice.

The ice lady replied, her voice also soft, "Oh, she was part of the Orphan Exodus. You remember that the King freed the children from the Enchanter?"

Agatha Ann remembered that part of the story. It was a tale all the children of Bright City loved.

"And to tell the truth, she never wanted to be in a hot place again. (You should see the bottoms of her feet. Talk about calluses!) Someone found her a place working in the Cold Storing Locker. And one day, because she did her job so well, the Marketmeisters appointed her to be the Coldmeister."

"YOU! YOU!" shouted Agatha Ann. "YOU WERE THE ORPHAN GIRL WHO SCREECHED AND SCREAMED AT THE WORST OF MOMENTS?"

"I certainly was. And do you know what I learned? I learned that the King really loves little girls with very loud outside voices!"

"Really?" said Agatha Ann, her voice soft again without her knowing it.

The Coldmeister shook her head yes. "And look at what has happened. Not many want to work here in this cold. But I am content and most happy, despite chilblains. I'm a worker for the Restoration by doing my cold job well. Can you keep a secret? I think the Cold Storing Locker is one of the most beautiful safe places in the whole City."

"THAT'S WONDERFUL!" Agatha Ann shouted, and this time she didn't even try to be quiet. A puff of airbreath bounced from her mouth and flew to the frosted pipes of the ceiling. And it was then, for the first time, that Agatha Ann looked around and saw how truly beautiful the inside of the Cold Storing Locker really was. Icicles hung like crystal pendants from the pipes and ceilings. Hanging lanterns cast a soft glow that shimmered with blue and yellow and white prisms of light on the walls and the floor and ceilings. Frost spangled every surface with its own kaleidoscope of colors. It was lovely, she thought, clean and a secret and with no dirt showing anywhere.

"Little girl with the very loud outside voice," said the Coldmeister, "I have a wonderful idea. Your outside voice is exactly what I need inside. Your airbreath must be very warm. When I do my paperwork, I have to take off my gloves and my fingers get stiff with cold. Why don't you come with me to my office while your mother is shopping and talk to me with your outside voice, and you can make the space where I work very warm indeed?"

And that is exactly what Agatha Ann did from that day on. She would knock on the door of the Cold Storing Locker, take a running start, and slide down the long icy corridor to the office of the woman in white. "HEY! I'M HERE!" she would shout, and then, in her very loud outside voice, she would tell the Coldmeister all the things she had done that day.

Puff after puff of steam airbreath filled the room, and the Coldmeister would sigh contentedly and smile and take off her gloves. Nodding her head as Agatha Ann chattered, she would quickly finish her paperwork.

When the butchers came about the meat, or the ice-chippers to inquire about bagging the ice-chips, or the freeze-dryers to discuss the timing of the drying, the Coldmeister didn't even have to remove her ear-muffs. She would simply say to Agatha Ann, "Would you repeat that for me?" And Agatha Ann would use her very loud outside voice to tell the Coldmeister what the others had said.

If the woman couldn't hear, she would say, "Louder, child! Louder!" And Agatha Ann would repeat, but in an even louder outside voice, "HOW MANY STRIP STEAKS?" or "A TON OF ICE CHIPS HAVE BEEN BUNDLED!" or "WE CAN'T FULFILL THE BEEF JERKY ORDERS! HOW MUCH MORE SHALL WE SCHEDULE?" And the lady in white would smile again and answer all the questions.

Strangely, the more the little girl used her loud voice inside when she was supposed to, the less she used her outside voice inside when she wasn't supposed to. One day the Marketmeisters came to Agatha Ann's mother and said, "We hear very good reports about your daughter. We hear she has learned to use her outside voice appropriately. We would like to give her another chance in the Mercantile Exchange. She needn't sit in the cold any longer."

Agatha Ann's mother was pleased. The vendors and buyers were pleased. So once again Agatha Ann carried the shopping basket for her mother, and enjoyed the free oranges when they were in season, and placed her saved pennies in the Sharebin. The windows no longer rattled when she came marketing. The dealers of wares no longer covered their ears when she spoke. And her mother was never again embarrassed by her very loud outside voice used inside.

But unknown to all the others, Agatha Ann really preferred to stand at a certain door where most people never knocked, enter the inside chamber all dazzlingly white upon white, take a running slide down the slippery icy corridor, grabbing an icicle to suck as she whizzed past, and then talk as loudly as she pleased while the Coldmeister did her paper-work. For Agatha Ann had found what everyone seeks, a place to be her-self, where one person at least, one very important person, cared that she could do what no one else could do. And, strange as it might seem to some, it was here in the cold that she was always warm.

Peril at Burning Place

Hero kicked the ashes at his feet. Having walked Amanda to the mouth of the path that led through the Garbage Dump, he now stood in the ashen field of Burning Place. She was making another night Crossing, and he was uneasy. With so many power-outs, the dark things had became bold.

"Amanda," he asked, "do you have to go at night?"

Yes. She was eager to arrange a Great Park transport, so that the remaining muddy play plazas could be transplanted and provide no more ammunition for riots in the streets. She and Ranger Commander had agreed to this haste.

"You know better than to worry about me," she chided, buttoning the collar of her blue runner's jacket. She knelt to tighten the strap that secured her felt running boots. "You know I can detect the deceits as well as any. It is a Crossing Again, which I have made countless times, and I am not afraid. I am never out of the company of the King."

Hero grinned at the confidence in her tone. Even in childhood, Amanda had been sure, sure of her gifts and sure of the strength she derived from being sister to the King.

"Well," said Hero, teasing, "don't go too far without a weapon. You've obviously left yours somewhere else." He pulled his silver-bladed woodsman's hatchet from its sheath and offered it to her.

Surprised, Amanda patted her belt. Sure enough, it was empty. She turned, searching the ground. Had she set it aside here? No. Where could she have left her hatchet? How could she be so careless?

Hero laughed, glad to best her for the sake of the old rivalry between them. "Well, I see you don't do everything perfectly. Take mine. You can't make Crossing Again, and at night, without a weapon." He paused, thinking, then said, "In fact, why don't you keep it for the rest of your life?"

With one hand Amanda pushed the hair back from her temple. She was not happy about being dependent upon someone else's gift for protection. Carelessness was not a good sign and could endanger many. And she had an uneasy feeling about where this conversation might lead her. There had been other comments from Hero that she had successfully ignored.

Croiee! Croiee! the watchtower horns blasted. Day's End was approaching. The signal warned any lingerers still outside the walls that night was near and dark things would soon be creeping out of the Dump. The carillons of the City had rung an hour before, calling people from work to home and family and dinner.

Amanda fastened Hero's hatchet in her belt and pulled up her collar against the evening cool. "I'll keep it for Crossing," she said. "But I can't possibly keep it for life."

Hero, muscular and agile, stood still beside her. He was no longer the lad who had fled from the Enchanter's orphan dragnet, believing old folk tales about a place where trees grew. He had worked with all the fighters of the Resistance, and now was a Ranger Leader in the Restoration. He was one of the King's choice men.

"Amanda?" he said softly. There was a question in the way he pronounced her name. To keep her from running along before she had answered his inquiry, he placed his hand gently upon her arm.

The young woman, as brave as the man beside her, as dedicated to the work of Restoration, dared not look into his eyes. She knew she must not hesitate in her answer. For in her heart, Amanda loved Hero as much as she loved any who were dear to her. He was part of the memories of her youngsterhood. They knew one another's growing, and she was proud of who he had become.

It was Hero who had befriended her at the time of her greatest failure, when through disobedience she had brought fire to Great Park. It was he who had led her back again through the Circle of Sacred Flames to the King. And as she had once taught him the ways of the fields and forests, it was Hero who had taught her the ways of the streets. Together they had infiltrated Enchanted City to fight in the Underground Resistance. Together they had stood at Burning Place and watched death and darkness and, at last, New Day Rising. Assured as she seemed, she had always drawn strength from his strength. Never wavering in the King's cause, Hero was a brave and loyal subject of the Kingdom.

To look at him now, and to see him deeply, would show that he was alone and needing a stay-beside person for the rest of his life. Her resolve would weaken. But it was her very seeing, this gift of inner sight, that insisted she refuse him. She was of the meadows and streams. Her heart was firstmost in Great Park. With clarity, she knew she would never be able to stay-beside him for the rest of life, because he was of the City. This place of work and struggle and frequent disappointment was firstmost for him.

"Hero," she answered, still avoiding his glance, her eyes downcast. "You love me because I am the friend of your childhood. You love me because I am of Great Park, and that place now fills you with home-longing. The work here in the City is hard and tiring. You love me because you know me and are comfortable in knowing me. But . . . but to stay-beside one another for life—this, this will never be. It is not meant to be. I know it. I can See it. You must trust my Seeing."

He pulled her closer, and though she had grown tall, he was taller still. Lifting her chin with his hand, her eyes now met his. Behind them, the sun rolled downward, darkening behind the flying banners, the flags and towers of Bright City. Clouds bowed, bumping before the display of another Day's End.

"Amanda," he said. "I am not going to beg. Just tell me. Tell me that you don't love me. If you say so, I will never speak to you of this again."

Gently she drew away and faced the Garbage Dump, then walked a way down the path. He knew her too well. She could not say the words to him. She could not say, "I do not love you" without his knowing that she lied.

A little beyond his reach, she turned to gaze at him. Her words sounded firm, slightly harsh, even to herself. "You love what you cannot have and don't love what you can have that is far better than the love that you do love. You must understand: I never want to talk about this again!"

Amanda turned with such determination and started to jog so quickly into the Garbage Dump that Hero was convinced she had meant what she said. All his persuasions would never change her stubborn mind. He watched her run away, not waving farewell, not calling out the words of coming and going that city workers always spoke, "To the King! To the Restoration!" And Amanda was too far away too fast for Hero to see that tears streamed down her cheeks. She had done a hard thing that hurt her as well as her valiant friend.

He had been refused. Despair flooded him. How could he continue the tiresome work in Bright City alone? He needed someone to stay-beside him for life to make the tasks bearable, to make the disappointments lighter, to share the joys and satisfactions. He needed someone like Amanda who always saw the King, someone to whisper Sighting when his own Seeing was dim. If she did not love him, who could?

Raw with disappointment, aloneness churning in his soul, Hero wandered westward around the wall to Burning Place. There was another Watchgate Entrance on this side of the wallwalk. Dark was near, and nightlife would soon come creeping. He dare not stay outside the gates without his hatchet. Seasoned warrior though he was, fighting off deceits without weapons would leave him vulnerable to treachery.

Croi! Croi! the horns blared. He must go in. The gates would be closing. Yes, yes, he thought. Just a minute. Just a minute to absorb this blow. He called out, "Watch! Watch!" just to let the Rangers in the tower know a lingerer was still outside.

How appropriate. His heart burned with disbelief that she could refuse him so finally, and here he was standing in the ashen field. Angrily he kicked the soot at his feet. Gray puffs rose, then settled. He kicked again and again.

This is the place where dreams die, he thought grimly to himself. He recalled the awful time when the King had been dragged from Traffic Court, a condemned man. He could almost hear the jeers of the fire priests, their bells jangling, the screams of the people of Enchanted City, the howling laughter of the conniving Enchanter.

In his mind's eye he saw the flames around the burning pyre blaze higher and higher, the form of the King thrusting and shadowed in the fiery torture. He felt again the evil darkness that had descended on that night to end all nights, when hope was gone and the people of Enchanted City gathered and knelt weeping or stood stunned and silent in the ashes of this terrible field.

Clck-ck-ck-ck-ck-ck-ck. Something clattered beside him. Something cold caught his ankle, wound around. *Clck-ck-ck-ck-ck-ck-ck.* What? It looked like a chainroot that had just sprung out of the ashes. Hero tried to yank away, but the tether held firm. If only he had his hatchet.

A wind swirled, blowing ashes wildly around him. He was blinded by the gray dusky fog. "Watch! Watch!" Hero cried. Too late! A deceit of sightlessness. He could no longer see the last rays of Day's End, or the lightlamps which the Rangers should begin to fire upon the walls at this hour. One last horn warning should blare, but the deceit muffled sound, and he could hear nothing. Hero knew, seasoned warrior that he was, that he was in for a struggle.

"WATCH!" he shouted at the top of his lungs. Was no one listening?

"S-s-s-s-s-scarboy!" hissed a low voice from somewhere close. "S-s-s-s-s-scarboy!"

His old childhood name. Couldn't the dark things do better than that? That old name no longer frightened him. He was not a child, terrified of Branding or haunted by deathdrums. As a child at Branding he had struggled so, his face had been seared by a Burner with a hot iron. It was the Enchanter's mark for all to see. But the King had healed his scar at New Day Rising. He was a King's man, and the King had taken away the scar that had always shamed him.

"My name is Hero!" he shouted. "I am a King's man!" No, if the dark things were going to strike fear into his soul, they would have to do better than this. But he must get free from this tethering root.

From out of the thick ash fog, something sharp jabbed him in the back. A poker in the hand of a Burner. The young man tried to swing round, but the tether tripped him. He stumbled, ducked, swung again, hoping to catch the handle of the prod, to wrest it from his invisible adversary and have a weapon in his own hand.

"Ooff!" Something hard hit the back of his knees. Hero stumbled forward. The tether yanked him short, and he tripped to his knees. The deceit over his eyes thickened. He was alone at Burning Place with no one to fight beside him, no one to cover his hindside.

"I am a King's man!" he shouted. "It is not dark yet! This is only a deceit."

"His-s-s-s-s," said the whispering voice. "That may be. But s-s-s-s-still you cannot s-s-s-s-see. Scarboy!" The jab again, this time harder. They were playing tough games.

There was silence, then a slow beat began, soft, ominous: *Oo-mb-pha . . . oo-mb-pha . . . oo-mb-pha . . .* The gathering drums, signal for dark things to draw near. Hero located the sound. From there, and there, and over there came the drumbeat. Three beaters at least. Then waiting, silence still, only the drums signaling, calling dark things forth. Then came the familiar voice in his ear. A voice filled with terrible knowing.

"She does not love you. She does not love you. No. No. No."

A wind blew across Burning Place, cold, paralyzing. Hobbled, sightless, alone in this field of ashes, Hero felt a knife of terror, like an ice-pick, thrust into his heart. The enemy knew his deepest, most hidden fear.

"Watch!" he cried, now on his hands and knees. "Watch!" But his voice was choked. He no longer believed he could be heard. He no longer believed that anyone wanted to hear him. Huddling, he drew up to his knees, ducked his head to protect it, and covered his neck with his hands to ward off the blows and jabs. Something pushed his face into the ashes. Soot smashed against his eyes, his ears, his nose. He breathed ashes into his lungs. The stink gagged him. He tried to scream. A shuddering gasp sucked up the ash into his mouth.

Suddenly he was so tired, tired of the work, tired of the power-outs, tired of city people. He was tired of this life of struggle. It was true: Amanda did not love him. Could not love him. No matter how hard he fought, no matter how much command he assumed in the Restoration, she would never love him.

Something soft pushed against his side, something gentle and kind. Was there aid? Hero leaned for a moment against this invisible comfort. Then the soft thing whispered beside him, intimately, like a friend, "And you don't see the King so well, either, do you?"

Hero jerked away from the pretender. First, the deepest fear. Now, the most terrible truth. Others in the Restoration saw the King with ease. Even Little Child had known the Streetsweeper in the middle of the mobbing riot. All Sightings came to Hero by hard-won discipline and determined effort. How could he be a worthy Ranger Leader if he did not Sight the King?

In just a few moments, outside the city walls, with night descending, he had been reduced to terror. He knew the Rule: It is dangerous to be a One Only. He regretted his carelessness.

The worst deceit of all came pressing hard against him: slumber-longing. His eyes felt heavy. He could hardly push up to his knees. Poke. Prod. Club. The dark things harassed him as he moved. Up. Get up. He must fight against this staggering weight. Oh, to be still, to give way, to cease. No. Up. Up. Stand. Stand. He tried to cry, "Watch!" once more, but the ashes clogged his throat. He spit to clear his mouth. He gagged on the vile choking stuff.

The King . . . he was so tired. The King . . . sleepneed like a drug paralyzed his mind. The King . . .

Heartsickness clutched his chest and squeezed. Hero moaned. He stumbled again, righted himself. Nightailment grabbed the back of his neck and would not let go. Pure terror now throbbed in his blood, at his temples, with each heartbeat. He fought back with the last ounce of his will: *This is not a real fatigue. This is not a real darkness. There is sound outside this deceit and light.*

"To the King!" Hero cried, desperate.

The voices whispered back, "But the King is not here. He will not come."

Hero cried again, one last time. "To the King! To the Restoration!"

Then there was a yammering. He was shoved in the dark by things he could not see. Then a voice, another voice—above the commotion, or beneath it, or behind it—said, "I am near."

I am near! Who had spoken? Hero strained to hear. Was it the King? Or was it another deceit?

Hero coughed. He spat ashes out of his mouth. "To the King!" he cried again.

Again the new voice, but this time laughter, a laugh Hero knew and loved. This was not a mockery. This was not a taunting jeer. It was the laugh of a conqueror, and it called, "I am very near. Nearer than you know. Do not be afraid."

How often had he heard that laugh before, heard it the first morning of New Day Rising, heard it at Burning Place, this very place when the King's fire had flamed after despair, here where the holy light had been tossed high above the heads of the dancers, and here where Great Celebration had finally come to the City. The King had lifted the evil enchantment through absolute power, and through conquering joy. Joy was here at Burning Place again. Now. At this very moment.

Hero saw a light tumbling high, piercing the deceit of sightlessness. He could hear the hum of battle thrilling in the air above him. The deceit of soundlessness had been destroyed. A command came, "Catch!"

He grabbed the falling, turning handle of a fighting hatchet that had been tossed his way.

Then the King's voice again, "To arms! I am at your hindside."

Hack! Hero swung widely in front of him. *Hack!* Hero could now see dark things hunkering down in the faint last rays of Day's End. He could see lightlamps burning brightly on the wallwalk.

Croiee! Croiee! As soundlessness fled, he could hear the watchtower horns blaring the last warning before nightfall.

Hack! Hero cut away the entangling chainroot that trapped his ankle. He heard laughter behind him and turned to see the King, young and battle-strong and confident, parrying with two Burners who were attempting to inch across the ashfield toward the Garbage Dump.

Croi-Croi! Croi-Croi! The horns blasted in double time, calling Rangers to the battle. From the city, men and women bearing torches, approached the circle of combat in which the two warriors stood back to back.

Take that and that! Hero bested one Burner of a poker. He thrust with another deft blow, and a Breaker's cudgel fell.

Dark night came finally, but light flamed in the circle of protection. All the Enchanter's hoard trapped within the torches scrambled to scurry beyond its reach, beyond the sure thrusts of the King's hatchet, beyond the now furious backwhacks of Hero's weapon.

"Is the gate secured?" the King called, not wanting any of the fleeing nightlife to creep through to the city.

"Gate secured!"

"ADVANCE!" the King commanded.

With that the fighting men and women, holding the ends of their torches in one hand, began to move the shadows and the power pretenders back, back, back, toward the Garbage Dump.

Realizing they were outnumbered, the terrorists turned and ran, yowling and wailing. They had crept out against a One Only, but they had been bested by the King and his many.

Sweat stood on the foreheads of the combatants. They wiped it off and straightened their garments. The King thrust his hatchet in the ashes to clean it. The silver on his clasp flashed in the flare of the torches.

"Lost your weapon?" he asked.

Hero cleared his throat. He knew it was perilous to be outside the walls at night, alone, without a fighting hatchet. The King must wonder why he had allowed himself to be caught at such risk. He took a deep sigh, "Ah—lent it to Amanda. She's Crossing tonight. Think she'll be all right?"

The King grinned, raised his hands at his side, and shrugged his shoulders. "Amanda? *You* can't be worried about the Princess Amanda!"

Right, Hero reminded himself. Amanda always made Crossing successfully. In fact, she might be approaching Great Park already. A little humility was necessary: it was he who had required protection. Facing the King, Hero grinned back and raised his hatchet above his head. The King lifted his, then crossed the neck of the other handle, hooking the two into one. A joint rescue.

"How long were you beside me?" He tucked the hatchet into his belt.

"Oh, since your first watchcry."

Hero groaned. Why was Sighting so hard for him? He said, "I guess I just couldn't see you."

"No," said the King. "It was more that you weren't really looking for me."

They walked back toward Watchgate Entrance, the Ranger Protectors falling into ranks behind them. Hero paused to view the procession of Rangers climbing toward the City, their torches flaming. He thought, "These are my people, the ones to whom I will always belong."

The King threw his arm around the shoulder of his fellow fighter and smiled. "You've always had trouble at Sighting, haven't you? A good fighter. A brave worker. A choice leader. But seeing?—well, that's more Amanda's task. Right?" The King was speaking out loud Hero's most secret, most terrible truth.

"Listen to me," said the King, as they stood together outside the gate.

Fellow and sister fighters passed and called, "Night's good eve!" "Good job done." The Ranger cry sounded from the Surround, "To the King! To the Kingdom! To the King! To the Kingdom!"

Hero looked into the face of the King and knew everything His Majesty had said was true. He was often too busy with other important things to really look for the King.

"Listen to me," said the King again. "Though I have many things to do in many places, I am always near.

"In battle, I am at your hindside.

"In duty, I am at your working hand.

"In slumber, I bend to protect you.

"In loving, I am your heartsong.

"In Great Celebration, I am always, always with you."

The King grasped Hero's shoulder with his right hand and said clearly, "You do not have to see me to find me. You do not have to hear me to know my words."

As the Ranger men and women passed, they began to sing, "He is always near. The King is always beside you. In battle, at your hindside. In duty at your working hand. . . ."

The Song of the King traveled with the singers through the gates, into the night, and through the streets of the City, now preparing itself for slumber. As the Rangers passed, people opened their windows or came to their doors or paused in the streets on their way home and all joined their voices in the song. "In love I am your heartsong. In Great Celebration, I am always, always with you."

When all the company had passed through Watchgate Entrance, and the torches flamed now in the lightlamps upon the wallwalk, and the sound of the Song of the King was being carried throughout all Bright City, Hero heard his name called.

The Ranger Leader turned, making ready to go his separate way. "Yes, your Majesty?" he replied.

The King answered, "Hero. There is one who loves you." Then he too was gone into the streets of the singing City, into the ease of nightrest, into this good eve. And Hero remembered well the lesson he had learned again and again through his living: Though alone, he was never really alone.

Sighters Are Not Afraid

Croi—Croi! The horns from the Ranger watchtowers blasted their message. *Croi—Croi!* Two short blasts meant that someone was making Crossing.

Little Child had spent the days since his own Crossing learning the ways of Bright City. Soon he would choose to become an apprentice to a Master Teacher who would teach him how to take his place in the Restoration. If only he knew exactly where he belonged. Was he a player, or a dancer, or a song-maker, or a craftsperson? Was he a trader, or an artisan, a cabby, or a crewmate? What was his special place?

Croi—Croi! the horns blared. "Crossing! Crossing!" workers around him cried.

Little Child hurried to the watchgate that faced the Garbage Dump. Since his own Crossing, he had loved being part of these welcomings. How well he remembered the heartening hurrahs that had greeted him from the walls of Bright City.

From the storage barrels beside the gates, he grabbed a colorful streamer bound around a slender pole. Tucking its handle into his belt, he scrambled hand over hand up one of the knotted hanging ropes, his feet pushing hard against the stonework and propelling him upward. At the top, standing on the wallwalk, he saw a large caravan of carts and wagons lumbering from the Garbage Dump. They were being pulled by great beasts of the forests. A troop of Rangers in working blues plodded beside the buck elks and deer stags, their stately heads of horns bowing and straining mightily against leather halters and harnesses. From this distance, the cavalcade looked to Little Child like a moving line of greenery. The wooden vehicles were piled high with bushes and trees.

The boy wondered: How in Great Park did they avoid the pit-traps and bog-mires? How did they get all those heavy carts up the mountains of refuse? How many days had they been traveling across the Garbage Dump? How had they avoided coming under the Enchanter's power?

"L.C.!" a voice called from below. Hero was vaulting effortlessly up the rope ladder to the wallwalk. "Found you," he grinned. Wrapping one strong arm around his younger brother's shoulder, he said, "Ah, you see. Great Park comes to Bright City."

"But how—but how—?" stammered the lad, still amazed.

"How did they get this loaded caravan across that most perilous path?" Hero threw back his head to laugh at Little Child's obvious amazement.

"Folks always wonder. First of all, this is not a Crossing Alone. Those are the hardest. This is a Crossing Again—a very different journey, believe me. Second, everything is under Ranger Protection. There are a dozen to fifteen Rangers guarding the Great Park caravan. The forest beasts themselves are canny in pathlore. They can sense danger. And thirdly, there—" He pointed with his finger. "That's probably the biggest reason we can move earth and forest across the Dump."

Little Child spotted a slim figure arched on the outside of a cart, vigorously retying a rope to secure a tree bending far over the side and dragging its limbs in the dirt. The figure deftly kicked back, down and out of the way of the wheels. It brushed its hands, then shook out a wild shock of hair, which glowed in the sun like a field of summer wheat and could be seen even from the wallwalk.

"Amanda," pronounced Little Child. He began to unroll his brilliantly hued streamer.

"Yes, Amanda. Amanda scouts the paths. She knows which paths are shortest and which flat places are deceits. The princess is not afraid of the Enchanter or his men, and he knows it."

Little Child was amazed. "She-she's not afraid of the Enchanter?" The streamer on the pole hung limp from his hand and curled on the wallwalk like a bright cloth puddle. Wasn't that dangerous? Wasn't that overconfidence?

Hero's eyes grew pensive. His smile faded, and he became serious. "No. She's not afraid. And I'm not afraid for her. Amanda is one of those rare workers who always sights the King." A slight twinkle flashed in his eyes. "Go ahead—ask her some day. I know what she'll tell you. She'll look at you with deadly seriousness and she'll announce: SIGHTERS ARE NOT AFRAID. As though—as though everyone saw the King all the time in every place. But go ahead—ask her for yourself."

With that Hero turned, caught up the vaulting rope, angled himself backward over the stones and began easing himself down the side.

"Aren't you staying for welcoming?" Little Child called as he descended. The older brother paused, his feet braced against the wall and looked up. "Can't stay. Gotta make sure those sites are ready for all this greenstuff. Tell Amanda hello for me." And he was gone.

Strange, thought Little Child. It was not like his brother to hurry off without a teasing word of greeting to his old friend. The boy looked over the wallwalk, and there she was. Amanda—striding with sure steps toward the watchgate, brushing dust and soot from her blue garments, stamping her boots on the path.

The other workers on the wallwalk were crying, "Hurrah!" They were waving their pennants. The Ranger horns blew their signal.

Little Child lifted his streamer up and above his head. It curled and unfurled in greeting, catching puffs of wind in its slender sail of color. "Amanda!" he cried out, glad to see her. "Amanda! Up here! Up here! It's me. L.C.!"

The young woman searched the wall with her eyes, spotted his flying signal, then saw the boy. Although her face was streaked with smoky smears, her eyes flashed joy. "Hey, Babykeeper!" she called, teasing him with another nickname from Great Park days. "You're just the fella I want to see."

Carts bumped and jostled beside her, pushed and shoved by the Ranger command into the city. Amanda ducked this way, then that. In a great hubbub of bustle and business, workers unloaded the plants and bushes and trees, then unharnessed the great stags and bucks so they could water in the troughs and roll on the grass and graze in the soft fields outside the city walls.

Amanda hoisted a set of harnesses to her shoulder and called out, "Meet you at the scrub-up," then disappeared beneath him through the watchgate.

He furled his streamer around the pole, clambered down, and tucked the banner back in the barrel. When he spotted Amanda again, she was in the crowd of travelers washing at the fountain just inside the gate. Her face and arms and hands dripped from the refreshing scrub. She turned quickly, flicked water at him, laughed, shook her hands, waved to her Ranger friends, grabbed Little Child's arm in her own, and hurried him off. "Well, my job is done. A most successful Crossing, if I do say so myself. And now, you and I are going to hunt for Lost Children."

Whoa! thought Little Child. "I-I don't know anything about hunting for Lost Children!" He stopped and pulled away from her grasp.

She grabbed his elbow again and began marching him along. "That's why you're coming with me. I'm going to teach you how. Everyone's been so busy restoring things that no one has time to go on Lost Children

Hunts. And we've got all kinds of lonely, hungry, scared little kids hiding in the dark places that still remain in Bright City. Today, I decided to do something about it. You and I are going to go hunting."

Little Child knew it was useless to argue. Once Amanda made up her mind, her determination was fierce. He noticed that the direction signs warned, "Moire Oxan Ahead: Caution is Advised."

He pulled his arm away again. "Amanda, are we going to Moire Oxan? I haven't been there yet. Hero says we should be careful not to go there alone."

A yellow taxi honked its horn, *Harnk! Harnk!* The driver waved and called, "Amanda! Glad to see you back!"

Amanda saluted a greeting, "Hey, Bub!"

The cabby whizzed around the corner. *Harnk! Harnk!*

She turned her full attention to the boy, placing her hands firmly on his shoulders. "L.C. What is this? Are you afraid? You made Crossing Alone in one piece and in good time. You, of all people, shouldn't fear Moire Oxan."

"I-I'm always afraid of new places, particularly new dark places. I don't think I'm very brave."

The young woman looked at him sternly. She stared directly into his eyes and shook him a little with each word. "You must remember and never forget: SIGHTERS ARE NOT AFRAID. Come along. We have important work to do."

Little Child walked briskly to keep up with the hurrying Princess. Under his breath, he mumbled, "That's exactly what Hero said you would say."

She heard him. "What are you talking about? What did Hero say I would say? And when did he say it?"

They had approached the great crumbling tenements where the Enchanter once housed the starving poor of Enchanted City. Broken porches sagged. Windows were boarded, staring sightless. Chunks of sidewalks littered the empty lots where ugly junk with rusty nails and knife-like edges waited to snag and cut children at play. Yellow signs were posted on buildings: CONDEMNED! ENTER AT YOUR OWN PERIL! The very air seemed sullen. It couldn't be possible, could it, that anyone still lived in this desolation? Nothing green or growing could be seen anywhere. Little Child's heart felt cold; the Enchanter had places here in Bright City, after all.

Amanda motioned him to stop and scanned the surroundings for a moment. "So. When and what did Hero say?" Amanda never forgot things when she wanted to know them.

"At welcoming. He said you would say: SIGHTERS ARE NOT AFRAID. Are-are we going in there?"

"Yes, we are. At welcoming? I didn't see him at welcoming."

Again she steered Little Child's arm as they crossed the street. She pointed toward a dark, boarded building where someone had torn away the door at the entrance.

Little Child did not want to go in there, even with Amanda. "No, Hero said he had to make sure the sites were ready. Bu-but he said to say Hi to you, though." Little Child was stalling. "Amanda, Thespia says that Hero is a One Only. Why is he?"

He saw her eyes flash, anger pushing behind them, and he didn't know why. She only said, "You must ask Hero himself. Only he can give you the answer to that." She changed the subject. "Now we are going to concentrate on teaching you to hunt for Lost Children."

They approached the dark shanty building in silence. Amanda held her finger in warning against her mouth, listening. Little Child listened too. Far off he heard someone call out, "Yo!" . . . a workman calling to another, then the drone of a machine moving refuse. Taxis honked in the distance. Then very faintly, he thought maybe he heard the sound of a child crying. There was someone in this awful abandoned housing project.

"We are going to go in here," Amanda said. "We go in quietly, trying not to make a lot of noise. Lost Children are afraid. They hide from danger. We don't want to startle them by making them think we are after them. But we do want them to know that we are here. We will go into their dark place, find an unlocked room, and in not too-loud voices we will tell each other stories about the King."

"That's it?" Little Child wanted to know. "That's all? What if the Enchanter's men are hiding in the darkness?"

Amanda smiled at him, her grin crooked as though she knew something no one else knew. "Well, everyone loves a good story. Even the Enchanter's men." She punched his shoulder lightly, "Buck up, Babykeeper. You just may be better at hunting than you know."

Oh, Amanda, he thought. *This is how you hunt Lost Children? You go into a scary abandoned building and tell stories in the dark? Awwwww.* Well, he'd try it this once, but only because he couldn't get out of it. And he knew he wasn't going to like it.

"Now." The Princess looked at him. "Tell me what you know about Sighting the King."

Little Child thought. He knew that the King could enter through all locked doors. He knew that the King could bring light to dark places. He knew that you could see the King with your heart even when you couldn't see him with your eyes. He knew that the King was always near, especially in places where you were afraid. He recited all his knowledge softly for Amanda, who nodded her approval.

Then the two pushed back the wood that had once been nailed across the entrance. *Pom-m-m—pm-m;* it swung loosely back and forth. They ducked their heads. *Cr-ee-ee-k!* The floorboards were warped. What if one gave way? Amanda unsheathed her silver-handled hatchet and held it before her for the warm light it shed, for the comfort of its low hum. *Cr-ee-ee-k!* Another floorboard groaned. Little Child hunched his shoulders. Then—then he heard what sounded like dull scampering—rodents running before them! He put his hand on Amanda's back so as not to lose her. He tiptoed.

In the dark Amanda found another door and pushed against it. By the faint light of the hatchet, they could see that the room beyond was filled with cartons and old chairs, the rusty springs of a bed without a mattress, and a broken fallen table.

"Here, help me," she whispered. Together they pushed the junk to the sides of the room, then she sat down in the middle.

"Remember, L.C., the Lost Children hide because they are afraid. They have run away from cruel keepers and have not yet found kindness. Some of them are nightcrawlers doing odd jobs for the Enchanter. The only song any of them know is the chant of the Naysayers. They still remember the Enchanter's rule: THERE IS NO SUCH THING AS A KING. DEATH TO PRETENDERS! And they have all been taught that Seeing Is Believing.

"Br-r-r-r-r-r," she said in a louder tone. "It's cold in here. It's always colder in dark and boarded places."

Little Child had begun to shiver, but not just from the cold. He thought he heard someone cough in a room nearby. Who was that? Then he heard something shuffling in the corner.

"Well, L.C.," said Amanda, a little louder. "Do you know a story about any Lost Children?"

Hm-m-m-m-m-m, thought Little Child. Did he know any stories about Lost Children? Yes. He did know one story about a lost and frightened child who had escaped from Enchanted City and from beneath the Enchanter's gaze and power.

"I do know a story," he replied. "Once upon a time, not long ago and not far away. . . ." And Little Child began to weave the tale of two brothers, of himself and of Scarboy, who escaped together to find the place where the trees grew.

And the more he told, the warmer the room became and the more he warmed to the telling. And the more he remembered to tell, the brighter the light from the hatchet seemed to grow. Little Child told about Mercie and Caretaker. And the more he told, the less afraid he felt. Yes, he remembered. *I have always been good at telling stories.*

"Hagh-hagh-hagh." The cough was now in the room. Lumps and bumps began to crawl and creep out next from the walls. *Sproing!* A dim form plopped on the old bedsprings. The room was full of children.

Little Child told the story of how he learned to speak and of how the Young Man had taught him how to stand on his hands. He felt a tug on his arm, and the next thing he knew a little girl with a dirty face and matted hair was sitting beside him, wiping her nose on his sleeve.

A rough looking boy in raggedy clothes had scootched out of the shadows to sit with criss-cross legs on the edge of the story circle. "Cant'cha tell us one more story?" he pleaded in a gruff low whisper. "Just one more story?"

And Little Child understood that the more he told the stories about the

King and the King's people, the less fear he felt, the less fear was in the dark room. Amanda was right: SIGHTERS ARE NOT AFRAID.

Little Child looked at the dirty girl in front of him on the floor, and he told how Mercie had said, "Everyone in Great Park belongs to someone else." And kindness for her filled his heart. Little Child took her hand, very slowly and gently so as not to frighten her. "Do you belong to someone else?" he asked.

She wiped her nose on her filthy sleeve this time. She looked wide-eyed at him and shook her head no. A big tear slid down her cheek.

Behind him, he heard Amanda say softly, "In the Bright City, all the children belong to someone." He turned his head and saw that Amanda was holding a little toddler in her arms. The child had tucked its head in her neck and its thumb in its mouth and had gone to sleep.

The boy kneeling on the floor coughed again, then his stomach rumbled. Little Child noticed that a smaller boy stood beside the rough looking lad, and he coughed too and was the skinniest child Little Child had ever seen.

"One more thtory," the little one lisped. "Jutht one more thtory. . . ."

It was as though all these Lost Children had been hiding in this dark building, just waiting for a storyteller to come along.

Amanda shifted the baby in her arms. Its thumb stayed stuck firmly in its mouth. "Now," she said quietly to the Lost Children. "I have an idea. We are very hungry. I wonder if any of you are hungry too?"

They looked wide-eyed at her and shook their heads yes. They were hungry too.

"Perhaps," she suggested, "you would like to follow the storyteller and me out into the Bright City. It is a very safe place where we are going, and everyone is welcome at the table. Then when you've scrubbed up a bit and eaten, I think there would be time for one more story. You won't have to stay if you don't like it. But if you want to, you may. And I really think you might like to hear a story I know. It's called: Princess Amanda and the Dragon."

Without a single word, the children gathered their things to follow. They hoisted small bundles into their arms. One of them found an ax handle. The little girl with the runny nose hauled the baby's bag, an old pillow case. "Baby's stuff," she explained. The littlest boy put on another sweater. They were bringing with them all they owned. None of them smiled. None of them made any protests as they left the crumbling shanty building.

When the bedraggled little band stood outside the tenement, Amanda paused. *"Wh-e-e-e-et!"* she whistled with two fingers between her teeth. Soon a yellow taxi with a checkered side slid to the curb.

The cabby opened the backdoor, "Yessir, ladies and gents. Where'ja all want to go?" The Lost Children climbed into the back seat: the girl with the runny nose, the rough boy with his little brother, Amanda and the baby.

"I think, Bub, first we'll get something to eat. And then we need to find a very quiet place where I can tell a good tale.

"See," said Amanda from the back seat to Little Child in front. "That wasn't so hard now, was it? All your babykeeping skills worked just as I suspected they would. Mercie taught you kindness well."

Little Child smiled to himself. She was right. Babykeeping seemed to have a lot to do with finding hungry and dirty and mistreated children. And he suspected . . . yes, he suspected that he had discovered a place in Bright City. Yessir, right now he couldn't think of anything he would rather do than go into all the dark rooms, even the scariest dark room, and be a hunter. Hunter . . . hey! that wasn't such a bad name. He didn't feel much like a little child any longer.

Strange, but true, Amanda was right: SIGHTERS ARE NOT AFRAID.

Prima the Ballerina

Prima, the ballerina, worked so hard at dancing she even danced in her sleep. In the middle of the night strange poundings coming from her bedroom would waken her family. *Ffump . . . ffump.*

"She's doing it again," her sleepy mother would say to her father and poke him with her elbow.

"Will somebody stop that crazy girl?" moaned her older

brother groggily from across the hall.

"Hrrumph," her father growled as he crawled out of bed. Putting on his robe, he complained to his wife, "You're the one who named her Prima and who filled her head with all this nonsense about being the best."

Sure enough, when he opened the door to Prima's bedroom, there she would be, dressed in her warm pajamas, poised on her bed with the springs squeaking and creaking, exercising her classical ballet steps: *Plié. Tendu. Frappé. Échappé.* All the time she was facing her bedroom mirror even though she was sound asleep. *Ffump . . . ffump . . . ffump.*

Prima's goal was to be the best ballerina in the City. She wanted to soar in higher *jettés* than any other dancer. She wanted to turn round and round in amazing *fouettés.* She wanted to look more beautiful than all the others, to stun audiences with her grace. She wanted the spotlight. She wanted standing ovations. She wanted piles of flowers from admirers.

She practiced hours every day, and only left the Dance Studio when the Dancing Master turned off the lights and locked the doors. She ignored her strained muscles and the bleeding blisters on her feet.

Actually, Prima was not happy with the Dance Studio Company. She felt that the others were not as dedicated to the dance as she. None of them worked as hard. None had a dancer's body. Few had the long slender limbs or the high arched instep of the classical dancer's foot, or a light strong leap. She was sure only a few had dancer's rhythm. And she was absolutely certain that none of the others practiced in their sleep.

Except, perhaps, for Carney. Carney, a rich man's daughter, was the only other natural dancer in the corps. She danced as though she never stopped hearing the music. She danced easily, making difficult steps look as though she had never spent dedicated hours in the Dancing Studio. And she never acted as though she thought the other members of the Dance Company looked awkward and funny. She never tripped them when the Dancing Master wasn't looking or nudged them off balance. She never made snide comments about their appearance. That girl was too good to be true, and Prima didn't like her one bit.

Standing at the practice barre now, Prima could see Carney reflected in the wall of mirrors, laughing with a boy who had short legs and a very round stomach.

"Like this," Carney said to him, demonstrating the steps to a sequence. "Then like this." He tried to copy and Prima snorted at him. Out loud.

Carney and the rotund boy looked up and caught sight of themselves in the studio mirror. The boy giggled at himself, a jolly round gurgle. "See, I'll never be a dancer."

Carney laughed with him, put her arm around his shoulders, and said, "But you can learn to love the dance. That's the main thing."

Prima didn't like the way the two of them were having fun together. Then she caught a glimpse at her own face in the mirror. She was scowling. Quickly, she changed her expression. She opened her eyes larger. It was important to develop the habit of always looking lovely. She despised ballerinas who frowned and grimaced while working out. As a dedicated dancer, she spent a lot of time watching herself in these mirrors. Her mirror image showed her exactly how she did. If she kicked a leg above her head, so did her image. If she bent her knees, her image bent her knees.

Prima thought to herself, *Having a rich father doesn't mean you will become the best ballerina, does it? That's a matter of hard work and talent. And if you give your time away to others, you won't have enough for yourself, will you?* She noticed in the mirror that her smile was smug.

With Carney in the studio, however, Prima practiced even harder: *Ronds de jambe. Arabesque. Attitude. Développé. Glissade.* She vowed to be Prima, a soloist, a principal dancer—no, *the* principal dancer. She determined to work her body into the perfect ballerina's body. Stretch. Extend. Turn-out. Turn-out. *En pointe!*—up on your toes! *Ffump . . . ffump . . . ffump.* She worked so hard she went through a pair of ballet slippers every week.

"Entendé, class! *Entendé!"* The door to the dancing studio banged open. "Listen, class! Listen!" The Dancing Master came sweeping through, followed by a ragtag bunch of—*oh, no,* thought Prima—*more Lost Children.* The Dancing Master was always dragging these ugly ragamuffins to the studio. "Look vhut ve haf here!" he shouted, as though it

was the most delightful surprise in the world. "Ve haf new members for our dansing com-panee."

As Carney hurried to greet this scruffy crew, fury began to boil in Prima's soul. Now the Dancing Master would give these sloppy-footed missteps more time and her less. She never got the attention she deserved.

The Dancing Master continued, "Now, little vuns. You are here to study the danse. But Dance Studio Com-panee is not like other com-panees. Here, ve help vun another. Here is no stars. Here ve learn to danse for Keeng. Here, is best dansing vhen ve hold hands and learn steps together. Vhut? You understand all zees? Effry danse is part of Celebration for New Day Rising."

Standing at the barre, Prima snorted again. She had never seen more unlikely dancers in her life. They had no poise. No presence. They shuffled their feet. Their clothes were shoddy. Their ungroomed hair fell into their eyes. Shoelaces flopped on the ground. She could see them tripping on slipper ribbons. She could see them bumping each other in a *pas de deux* and stumbling apart. How would they ever stand on stage and command the attention of an audience?

"So vhut, Prima? You have somesing to say?" The Dancing Master had heard her snort. His eyes were stern.

Before answering, she insolently bent to adjust her leg warmers. Then she stood straight, smoothed her gauzy tulle skirt down around her leotard. Placing her hands on her hips, she forced a smile. "Yes, I do have something to say. How can anyone dance for the King when nobody ever sees the King?"

Everyone made such a big deal over the fact that the people of the City now lived daylives, that the King had lifted the enchantment that once forced people to work and play only at night. But what did she care? She had never seen the King (if there really was a King), and the only light that mattered to her was stagelight.

The Dancing Master spread his arms to the whole dancing class. "Is like vunderful game. The Keeng is alvays vit us. Ve cannot see. Ees in disguize. But. Alvays, he sees us. Und ve learn to find him. So. Ve danse alvays for Keeng. In Bright City, beliefing is seeing."

The trim man flipped up his wrists—like so. He bowed low, then executed a few quick steps and turns. The Lost Children clapped. He leaped into the air and twisted before his feet touched the ground. All oohed and aahed.

Except Prima. She pouted. The Master's leap was wonderful, particularly given the fact that he did it without warm-up time. Any professional would recognize that. But the ballerina hated it when anyone else received the attention.

The Dancing Master smiled at his students. "Is notsing. Notsing." He waved away their approval with his hand. "You see. Here in Dansing Studio, ze older help ze younger. Ze stronger help ze weak. Ze principal dansers help new dansers. Ve all learn to do best ve can. Ve make beautiful danse for Keeng."

Under her breath Prima mocked, *Is notsing. Is notsing.* Well, no one was going to make her partner with that fat boy and look ugly because of him. And she didn't care a whit about the King. To her, seeing was believing.

Prima leaned toward the barre again. In the mirror she watched Carney line the Lost Children against the far side of the studio. Quickly, joyfully, the other girl did a series of pirouettes, whirling like a top on her toes and tapping each child on the head as she passed. "Like this! and like this! and like this and like this! You too will learn to dance for the King!"

To Prima, the children in the mirror looked like cartoon clowns doing warm-up exercises. They would make a terrible ballet corps for *Swan Lake* or *The Nutcracker*. The only choreography that would work for them was one for a new work someone would have to create—*Plump Sausages and Sticky Hot Cross Buns*. Prima chuckled to herself. The only way to become a success was to be concerned about yourself first! Look out for number one!

Her image in the mirror lifted her ankle to the barre and bent forward, stretching out her spine and calf muscles. Then Prima, the ballerina, did the same. She was so pleased at her own clever humor that she didn't even notice this odd shift in the practice sequence.

The days that followed were full of hard work. Prima was so determined to be number one that she began to sneak into the studio after everyone had gone home and the doors were locked. She had stolen a key from a hook in the Master's office. She danced in her sleep anyway, she might as well dance in her sleep here. She was tired of her family's complaints. They never had understood her desire to be the best.

Turning on the music, she had the whole room to herself. She watched her image flitting gracefully across the mirrors with no one else to spoil her positions or crowd her space or interrupt her concentration as she made dazzling passes.

But strangely, as the weeks passed, the harder she worked, the less satisfied she became. Her leg muscles were bunchy. She didn't like the way her face looked. She felt fat. Her neck wasn't long enough. Maybe she should change the color of her hair.

She noticed that Carney, though she spent precious practice hours helping the other children, seemed to grow more graceful, more lithe and carefree in her dancing. There was something joyous in the way she lifted her upper body. Something elegant in the way she tossed her head. Something breathtaking in the way she held a pose while leaping, seconds longer than any leap seemed possible. She had something that could not be imitated by another, though Prima tried sneakily to copy her form.

One night, after hours of frustrating private work, Prima's image in the mirror plopped down on the floor, ankles crossed, head in her hands. Prima followed. She just could not get it right. She felt like crying. In fact, she did cry.

Suddenly the door to the studio opened. Carney stood there, holding her ballet bag in her hand. "Prima? Prima? I was working late. But why are you crying? Can I help?"

So this was how her rival did it, the cheat. She practiced overtime.

Prima wiped her eyes. "I wasn't crying—but I just can't get it right. I'm so frustrated. It is always out of reach. I will never be a prima ballerina."

Carney put down her bag and sat on the dance floor beside her. "Prima. You're a wonderful dancer. You work so hard, harder than anyone else in the whole company—and yet . . . well, perhaps you work too hard. I think I dance the best when I forget myself in the dance. In some way we become a servant to the music."

At that moment, unnoticed by either of the two dancers, the mirror image lifted its head. A yellow light of envy flashed in its eyes. Then Prima lifted her head. "Wha—what do you mean?"

Carney smiled and handed the girl a tissue for the tears she said she had not been crying. "Once upon a time, when I was a little girl, an evil man, a very evil man came hunting for me. I was afraid he would catch me and keep me forever. So I ran away. And when I ran away, I became lost. Then a stranger, another man, but good and kind, came searching for me. He found me and he took away all my fears. When I looked into his eyes, I saw that he loved me. Prima, it was the King. I have seen the King, and he is the most wonderful and beautiful of men.

"I will never forget how terrible it is to be lost. And I promised myself I would always help children who were lost and afraid. Most of the children will never be great dancers. We all know that. But they are learning to lose their griefs and terrors in the movements. The music helps to heal them and gives them somewhere to belong. They, all of them, can be joyful dancers in the Great Celebration.

"And do you know what? Whenever I look into their eyes, I remember the gaze of the King. And I forget myself when I dance and try to make it all beautiful for him."

Carney paused. Prima had stopped listening. In fact, she had gone to sleep. Or rather, behind the two, the mirror image in a fit of disgust had put down her head and covered her ears with her hands to keep from listening. The ballerina had followed her example.

Sighing, Carney rose to her feet, found an old robe in an empty locker, and put it over the sleeping form. Then she wrote a note to the Dancing Master: *I am concerned about Prima. She chooses to be a One Only. And I don't think she knows the danger. To the King! Carney.* She turned out all the lights but one.

In the middle of the night, Prima woke. She stretched and began to exercise at the barre. "'I-have-seen-the-King,'" she mimicked Carney to her mirror image. "What a goody two-shoes! 'Prima-maybe-you're-working-too-hard.' I know what she's up to. She's pretending that she doesn't want to be prima ballerina to put me off my guard. Well, I'm not stupid."

The image in the mirror smiled. Prima smiled back. She turned three-quarters to the mirror. Her legs were beautiful and shapely. Her neck was long and willowy. What could have been the matter with her to think herself ugly? Certainly, she was just suffering from dancer's fatigue.

The image in the mirror performed a series of stretching exercises. Prima did the same. That was nicely executed. The image in the mirror bent deeply in *plies*. Prima bent deeply in *plies*. Yes! Gracefully done. The mirror image began leaping in the air—higher, then higher. Prima followed. That was the highest she had ever leaped.

Why, of course! If she just followed what the image did, she was brilliant. That was the secret for future success. She must give herself to following the image.

The mirror self turned in glorious circles, faster and faster. Prima did the same. One look told her that she had never danced so brilliantly or that her technique had never been so flawless. *I will follow you,* she thought. *Whatever you do, I will do. I will go wherever you lead me.* And not once did Prima think this to be odd.

Shortly, Prima quit Dancing Studio Company and joined the Imperialist Ballet Theater, which specialized in gala performances and was a company with many stars. And indeed, she became a solo ballerina. When the orchestra played, Prima remembered her mirror image and danced out the memory she saw in her mind. The spotlights dazzled her sight. When the audience gave her standing ovations, she curtsied just as she had seen the image in the mirror do, low and grandly like a queen. Yes, she was Queen of the Dance. During bows, the flowers of her admirers were piled at her feet, just as she had dreamed.

But she had no friends to call her own. And her family never called or came to see her dance. So she slept in a room filled with mirrors in order not to be alone. Her dressing room had a wall of mirrors. Her long sleek limousine windows were also mirrors, closing away glimpses of Bright City. She could never be, nor did she want to be, far from her own reflection.

In time, even when she wanted to, even when her body needed to rest, she could not stop dancing. Her mirror image demanded the motion. And though she danced beautifully, she never danced joyfully.

But Carney, Carney and the found children danced in the streets. They laughed when they bumped each other or tripped on their shoelaces. And because they had all kinds of bodies, fat ones and short ones and skinny ones and roly-poly ones, the old people who also wanted to learn to dance were not afraid to try. And because no one was a principal dancer, but all a part of the troupe, even self-conscious middle-aged ladies and men who had never learned to dance caught the infectious wonder of the steps and forgot to think about how funny they looked.

Much to the delight of the Dancing Master, Dancing Studio Companies were started all over the City. Here many people learned how to hold hands and how to help one another in the steps. Here people learned to love the rhythms of the New Celebration. Here they were taught the Dance of the New Day Rising.

And whenever they looked laughingly into each other's eyes, they saw, sometimes, without knowing that they saw, the loving look of their most beautiful King. For he is a King, after all, who takes joy when the people of his kingdom learn all the steps.

Taxi!

Taxi!" Amanda waved from the curbside, and the yellow cab with the checkerboard trim in which Little Child was training pulled to the curb.

"Hey, L.C.," Amanda called as she climbed into the back seat. "How's your taxi-lore coming?" She pulled the door shut.

"Where to, Bub?" said the cabby.

"Watchgate Entrance by the Garbage Dump."

Little Child turned. "Are you going to Great Park?"

"Yep. I'm out of here, and going home. Home to everything I miss. Going back to where the Kingdom really works."

Little Child knew that Amanda had never grown to love the City, no matter how many times she made Crossing. Great Park was her heart's true home, and though he was glad she could return to the place she loved, he would miss her happy spirit, her true insight, and her pluck and courage.

"I will miss you," he said aloud from the front seat. "Oh, Amanda, by the way. I-I don't feel so much like Little Child any longer. What do you think about a new name? What do you think about Hunter?"

Amanda smiled, leaned forward, punched his shoulder, and replied, "What a great name! Hunter. It's you."

Since hunting for lost children in Moire Oxan, the conviction had grown more and more that being a hunter was what Little Child wanted to do, was happiest doing. But he and Hero had both agreed that he couldn't do that job well until he knew every nook and cranny of the City. And what better way to learn the City than to become a MERCY ST. TAXI CORPS trainee?

Little Child agreed with Hero and the Chief Cabby that taxi training was the best way to learn street savvy. Then he could go anywhere in Bright City that he needed to go. When hunting in dark places, that knowledge would help to keep him safe.

But the truth was, not everyone could become a MERCY ST. TAXI CORPS cabby. These were the driving elite. Oh, you could become a van driver or a truck driver or a motor scooter driver, but the cabbies in those little yellow taxis were the best trained drivers around. They could always get you where you wanted to go.

First, a cabby-in-training had to attend lectures by the Chief about the past history of the Resistance, showing how the old underground strategy now formed the basis for the present operation. Next, time was spent learning the operations in headquarters, the schemes of city maps, the Central Dispatch Board, and basic cab maintenance from mechanics at the CORPS garage. Little Child studied the Chronicle of Sightings, past records of how the King had been sighted in the Enchanted City when he returned from exile. Finally, weeks were devoted to cruising the streets with a training cabby before going solo in trial tests on a motor scooter with a tracking clipboard strapped to the handlebar.

Little Child—that is, Hunter—was at this stage in his training. All the streets, cul-de-sacs, turn-arounds and backways had to be learned by heart. Cabbies needed to memorize which safe places were where in the five pendrants, where the healing house was found, the names of the grandma vigilantes in one's assigned taxi district, the quickest shortcuts to use when the traffic was busy, crowd control, how to dispatch radio commands, and how to decode horn signals. Cabbies also had to learn emergency first aid, Lost Child emergency evacuation rules, and rescue maneuvers in case of saboteur infiltration.

All of this comprised the taxi-lore, and MERCY ST. CORPS cabbies who passed their training tests were proud of the rigorous preparation that equipped them to drive a yellow taxi in the streets.

"Wh-when do you think you'll be back?" Hunter asked Amanda.

"Not sure," she answered. "All the Play Plazas are planted. You're learning taxi-lore fast and going on your own Lost Child hunts without me. Tell you what . . . I'll make sure I'm back when you're awarded your MERCY ST. TAXI CORPS certification."

Hunter groaned. That might never happen. He had doubts regarding his qualifications.

The taxi came to a stop near Watchgate Entrance. Eagerly Amanda hopped out of the back seat. Hunter walked with her to the gate, then climbed the ropes to the walkway to wave her off down the path. She only paused once in her homeward flight—"To the King!" she cried back to him. Watching her jog away, then disappear into the Garbage Dump, he was filled with an aching longing for the beauty, safety, and peace of Great Park. He almost shouted, "Amanda! Wait for me!"

Though Bright City was under Restoration, there were still many ugly places and many people who still did ugly things. Because the Enchanter's loyalists were always trying to breach the Ranger Surround, the city was never really safe. Since the day of mudslinging, the boy had longed for Mercie's cottage, for the fire on her hearth, for her voice. He ached for Caretaker and his jolly wisdom and his jingling prance along the forest paths. He wanted to be in the dance of Great Celebration, protected by the Sacred Flames. He wanted to live again where no Restoration was needed, but where Kingsways were always obeyed. He even missed tending to the babies.

"Hey, Bub!" It was the waiting cabby. He tooted his horn softly: *Harnk! Harnk!* "Can't stay here all morning. We got a Healing House to visit, remember?"

"Coming," Hunter called back. One of the MERCY ST. TAXI CORPS' missions was to transport people ready to leave the Healing Houses back to their own homes. This would be the first time he had actually visited a Healing House. But he was so lonely for the peaceful world he had once known, so filled with homelonging, that he gazed again for one short moment across the walls. He could vaguely see the green of Great Park in the hazy distance. In that welcoming place, all orphans belonged. There weren't packs of Lost Children roaming the streets, picking through garbage, as there were in the City. Why weren't more workers finding them? Why were they all so busy with Restoration projects that they weren't going on hunts themselves?

Harnk! Harnk! Hunter was down the rope and into the taxi.

The Healing House sat back from the streets in a walled garden. Immediately, Hunter felt it to be a place of peace and safety. It reminded him of the grounds around Mercie's Cottage in Great Park. There the flower beds and herb gardens were loved and tended. Here, he could see caregivers walking quietly beside those who were ill and healing, strengthening their weak steps, guiding them into patches of warm sunlight. Old people were pushed in carechairs along the smooth paths by young and gentle helpers. The wounded sat on benches beneath large sheltering trees.

"Lemonade?" A caregiver apprentice, carrying tall moisture-beaded glasses on a tray, took note of their arrival.

Gratefully they each grabbed a tall glass, and the cabby said to Hunter, "Wait here. I'll just go check and see about the transports ordered."

Three little children, somber and sickly, sat together under a tree. Their arms were skinny, their legs thin. More neglected children, thought Hunter. Bright City was full of poor and neglected and ill children such as these. How many could there be all together? Hunter sat down beside them to wait for the cabby. If only he could make them smile, just one little smile. "Say," he said. "Do any of you like stories? I know a wonderful story about a King."

None of the three answered, but hung their heads shyly and lowered their eyes, twisting their healing house gowns in their hands.

"Well, I like stories about the King," said Hunter to himself. "I know a true story, a story about someone I know—a little girl who one day met the true King." And he began to tell them the story of "A Girl Named Dirty," the girl who loved living with pigs more than living with people and how she met the King in disguise and how he invited her, filthy and naughty as she was, to dine with him. "Come, come with me," the King had said. "Be my special guest at the banquet table."

As Hunter told his story, the day grew softer, the sun felt warm but not hot, the roses in the garden waved their rosy scent, and unhappiness seemed to vanish with the day's breeze. Hunter himself felt a little better. "So the pig girl left her pigs for the sake of One she loved. And she became Cleone, the clean one, who had a tender place in her heart for all things ugly because she knew a King who could find something beautiful in every garbage heap. The End."

The children had drawn closer to his side, one had propped elbows on the teller's knees, one had tucked a hand into his arm. The little girl lifted her eyes to smile and lisp, "That thure wath a good thtory."

Behind him, to his surprise, hands clapped in soft applause. "Very good tale," said a quiet voice. Hunter turned quickly to see a man who was wearing the white jacket of a healing house worker. Hunter knew the wonderful voice at once; it was like a mountain brook falling over a stony riverbed, like wind blowing in the tops of trees. The man's eyes were bright, his back tall and strong, his hair glinted gold in the sunlight.

"Little ones," he said to the three children. "Caregiver is looking for you. Noontime high. Lunch for you all, and then rest and quiet." Grinning, he held out empty arms, then suddenly flipped upside down and started walking expertly on his hands. Silver-wrapped sweettreats fell from his pockets. The children laughed, scrambling in delight to gather the prizes. Hunter remembered that joy was always part of Kingsways—

perhaps the best medicine of all. And his own heart ached a little less to hear the sound of laughter.

Flipping upright again, the man knelt to give the little ones a hug. They nestled in his arms, patted his face, pressed their cheeks against his, and then walked carefully but obediently across the grass to the Healing House, clutching the shiny gifts in their hands. Hunter felt as though he too had been comforted.

"Do you work in the Healing House?" the boy asked.

"Yes, when I can. I love to work with the healers. We do good things together." The man smiled, and the boy was grateful to notice that all the sadness he had seen on that angry day of mudslinging was now gone from his eyes.

Just then the cabby bustled out the door and hurried to meet them, shouting as he walked, "Hey, kid! Got three transports—one for the front seat, two for the back, plus their stuff. Find something else ta do this afternoon! No room!"

"He can spend the afternoon with me," replied the Healer.

"Sure thing. Thanks, Mistuh." Then the cabby was off, calling back over his shoulder to his trainee, "See you tomorrow for street trials. Ten o'high sharp!"

"He didn't recognize you," said Hunter in surprise.

The Healer replied, "No. Most people don't. But the ones who tell my stories seem to see me most. I hear you are becoming a hunter. I spend a lot of my time hunting Lost Children. You should see me frequently."

A brown bird sang on a bough above their heads. They both looked up. The bird seemed to bob its head in greeting and turned its eye sidewise to see them.

"Let's go have some lunch," said the Healer. "The cook at this Healing House is an artist. Then, if you'll finish rounds with me, we can find Thespia and join the Streetplayers later this afternoon. Sound good?"

A whole afternoon in the company of the King! Hunter was thrilled!

Later, on their way to join the Street Players, they walked across the city together. Hunter heard all the plans for the Restoration that the King was making. One day Moire Oxan would be a safe place, with sand piles for making castles and lots for stickball. All the Lost Children would be found and would tell stories themselves. Here, there would be a band shell where music would gladden hearts in spring and summer. There would be an outdoor market. Here they were planning a common garden with a bicycle track around it.

And the strange thing was, the more Hunter walked with the King, and the more the King talked about his plans, the more the boy could actually see what the King seemed to be seeing. Yes, here were sturdy houses being built. Yes, he could hear the sound of children playing, running to catch balls and climbing on the equipment. He could actually see in his mind the bicycle races and the women and men gathering in the outdoor market with piles of fruit and containers of garden transplants. He could hear the music of the band in the band shell. He could imagine the gardens with everyone working in the soil, planting and hoeing and weeding and sharing the produce.

The city really was Bright City, no longer sad-looking, or dilapidated, or dangerous. It was under Restoration, with much to be done, certainly, but much better than it had seemed to the boy since the mudslinging riots. The King was near. The King had plans. The King could see the end of Restoration. Hunter heard the watch cry, "The Kingdom comes!" And the sound of the repeated echo thrilled his heart once again. "Yes," he reminded himself. "The Kingdom comes!"

Soon they arrived at Play Plaza 10. Beneath its newly planted trees, the Players were practicing a new drama Thespia had just created. She called it *The Streetsweeper.* The Players preferred to practice their street theatre outside. All the actors were in the middle of reading the new script, and Thespia was sitting cross-legged on a park bench, scribbling and making re-writes. Her strawberry-blonde hair lay in damp curls around her forehead. She was hot from the sunlight and the work.

"No," she called. "That song just doesn't work here. Players, turn to Act One, Scene Three. Top of the page. CABBY read your line and then, let's put the Song of the Mudslingers here. Okay? Places. Taxi horns ready? Begin."

She nodded and fluttered her fingers in greeting to Hunter and the King when they entered, but she was too busy directing to pause. At that moment Hunter saw Hero entering the Plaza by the other side. He too liked to end a busy day at the City Drama Center watching practices, or here in the Play Plazas which were blooming with the green gifts from Great Park.

Perhaps it was because he was sitting beside the King, and all things were clearer, that Hunter saw the look Thespia gave to Hero when he entered. But for some reason, Hero seemed to be blind to her glance.

"Wonderful! Wonderful!" Thespia cried after the Players had finished their reading of Scene Three and sung "The Song of the Mudslingers." "Oh, it works so much better up front like this. How did you all like it?" She turned to face the King and Hunter and Hero, who was now standing behind their bench, and lifted her hands in inquiry. "So? What do you think?"

The three of them clapped roundly. Thespia bowed. The troupe bowed. The Most Beautiful Player of All held her hand for the actors to stay, then came and knelt before the King. "Oh, I hope you like this. I hope you really like it. I know it needs work. It's just beginning to come together. But I wrote it for you. I wrote it just for you."

At that, the King took her hand and put his head back and laughed. "Oh, Thespia! Only you could make an ugly incident like that into art. 'The Song of the Mudslingers'! I love it."

Delighted, relieved, thrilled at his pleasure, the young woman rose to her feet, stretched out her arms, and spun around to the players. "Do you hear him? He loves it!" In turn, they clapped for the King.

"Now wait," Thespia said excitedly. "Just wait. If you don't have to rush off, I'll show you something else we're working on. But first you have to get the picture. This is street theater, to be performed right outside the Play Plazas. We'll blockade the intersections against traffic and enact the mob scenes. There'll be dance, there'll be song. There'll be pathos. There'll be the taxi vanguard. This dance we're working on is called 'The Dance of the Push Brooms.' Players? Get your props. Please remember," she said to the King, pointing with her finger at him and at Hero. "Please remember that we are still working on this."

The dancers ran to grab push brooms, tied kerchiefs around their hair, and formed two lines facing one another. They began. *Push-push. Swish-swish.* Their brooms made a rhythm as they danced the steps in time.

Push-push. Swish-swish. They sang: "We are the streetsweeps, cleaners all. We push the push brooms, standing tall."

They swung around the broom handles, leapt from one standing broom to the next, grabbed them with their hands and swept in rhythm. *Push-push. Swish-swish. Step-step.* They sang: "Mudslingers warning. Come one day. You may be sweeping brooms our way." *Push-push. Swish-swish.*

At the end of the dance, the King stood to his feet and applauded. "Something good out of something bad! Hurrah! Hurrah for you, Thespia! Mud into art. A King's blessing on you!"

Hero cried, "Bravo! Bravo!"

And Hunter realized that he was laughing and cheering, and that he hadn't laughed or cheered for a long time.

The players were dismissed. They'd worked hard enough for one afternoon. Suddenly, the carillons began to chime: "Work's end. Work's end." People all over the City called good day to one another, made plans to meet tomorrow, and went away laughing and feeling satisfied that they indeed had done a good day's work.

"Well, we'll all be eager to see this production, I'm sure," said the King. Then with one arm he grabbed Hero by the shoulder and pulled him to his side and with the other arm he grabbed Thespia by the shoulder and pulled her to his opposite side. "Little Child—I mean, Hunter—and I are going to spend Day's End with each other. There are some more things I want to show him."

The King strolled toward the entrance to the Play Plaza, talking confidentially to the two beside him. Hunter, still seated on the bench, could barely hear his words. "Special but difficult assignment . . . wonder if you two would consider . . . something I can only trust to a very few . . . Song Studio."

Watching the three of them, Hunter saw that his brother and Thespia were a handsome match. The truth was clear: She loved the City as much as he. She would no more leave it to live in Great Park than Amanda would leave Great Park to live in Bright City. Indeed, it was Thespia, and only she, who could ensure that Hero would be safe from the dangers of being a One Only.

Hunter knew that the King was sending them on special assignment because he knew the ways of love, and how it takes time to find it. And how some folk need help in the looking.

The boy watched the King wave the two off, then return. "Ready?" the tall man called—and winked.

Together, they walked to the street. Hunter realized that all his home-longing was gone. He was glad to be here in this place, at this time, doing this work, with these people. A day of walking in Kingsways had helped him see Bright City as it was meant to be.

Standing curbside together, the King winked again. "A good day's work. Right?" Then he lifted his hand and cried, "Taxi!"

The Song Studio

Outside the Song Studio, Hero waited anxiously for Thespia. Inside he could hear the singers practicing their warming-up scales. There was a Song Fest this afternoon, and they were making ready.

Why had the King sent the two of them on this particular assignment? Usually Hero saw Thespia only at the Drama Center or when her troupe was performing Street Theatre. She was a beautiful and talented player, and although he admired her obvious gifts on stage, he had doubts as to her abilities on special assignment. She wasn't a Ranger Fighter. She wasn't a seasoned warrior. Sometimes special assignments were risky, and he wanted to know that his partner was skilled at coping with danger.

"Hello," said a voice at his elbow. It was Thespia, and he was struck again with her beauty. Good for the stage, good for street theatre, but what good would it do if things turned ugly? He hoped the King knew what he was doing.

"Well, hello to you. There's a Song Fest this afternoon," he said, explaining the noises from inside.

"Oh, good," she replied as they entered the door together. "I love Song Fests."

The two took seats in the middle of the Song Studio meeting room where many were gathering to take part in the festival. Musicians were practicing their instruments. Cellos leaned against supports, violins rested on felt cloths, music stands were scattered here and there around. A dais stood in the center of the room, where the performing musician would sing or play.

"Who is the Music Maestro here?" Thespia inquired.

Hero answered, "Someone new. I don't know him. The Voice Teacher, however is an old friend. Her name is Oka. She came hunting for me and my brother after we had escaped from Enchanted City. She was Orphan Keeper's Assistant before the Orphan Exodus. Mercie took Oka in hand, and she became a wonderful worker in the Great Park Nursery."

"Her voice must be remarkable if she's a Voice Teacher."

"Yes," replied Hero. "She has a beautiful singing voice. It's filled with the sounds of Great Park."

The room filled quickly. Musicians took their places in the central circles of chairs. They whispered breath into reed instruments and lovingly tuned the strings of violas and violins. They pounded the rhythm drums and listened for vibration levels. Harps were plucked, chimes were softly dinged, and trumpets gently bleated.

In the outside circles of chairs, invited guests eagerly found empty seats. Most people in Bright City loved the Song Fests, times when the music apprentices demonstrated everything they had been learning and invited the audience to join in the music making.

"Hero," asked Thespia. "Do you notice anything strange about all the people in this Song Studio?"

Hero glanced around him. What did Thespia mean?

"Everyone here is very well fed," she whispered.

In surprise, Hero noted that she was right. He had never seen so many well-fed people in one room. *Why?* he wondered to himself. *In Bright City, there was so much Restoration work to do that not many people had the luxury of putting on pounds.*

"And," Thespia continued, "there are no Lost Children here."

Lost Children who had just been found could always be identified. They were skinny and undernourished and had skinsores. They wore raggedy clothes and broken shoes and had straggly hair. And they were always hungry. Lost Children loved Song Fests and often found safety for the first time in the festivals.

Hero noted Thespia's powers of observation. Of course, he thought, she must have a developed the habit of scrutinizing audiences. But she was right: Everyone in this Song Studio looked well fed . . . too well fed. Everyone in this meeting room, besides Thespia and Hero, was grossly overweight.

Now in Bright City, there were many people of many different sizes. There were tall people and short people. There were round people and slim people. But it was strange that so many people in one place should all be so round. And it was strange that there were no Lost Children in the room.

The player had analyzed the difficulty in this Song Studio with exceptional deftness.

At that moment, a woman sat in the chair next to Hero. She actually sat on two chairs, and her children, three of them, all well on their way to becoming as heavy as she, occupied the last empty seats in this circle.

Ta-ta-ta-ta-ta-ta. A man dressed in a black silk shirt, neatly pressed pants, and a flowing cape was striking the music stand on the raised dais. His cape was lined with bright pink silk. He held his baton at ready until total quiet had settled on the room.

Thespia whispered, "Interesting. The Maestro isn't overweight at all."

Hm-m-m-m-m, thought the Ranger Leader. *Right again.*

The room hushed with anticipation as the Music Maestro lifted his baton, then waved it in airy curlicues to produce the richest sounds Hero had ever heard. Nothing jangled. No musician was behind or ahead of time. The music of all the separate instruments flowed into one another like stirred batter for a batch of the sweetest of chocolate chip cookies. Smooth and creamy the notes flowed. Just sitting and listening, Hero felt suddenly hungry.

"What a beautiful sound," he whispered to Thespia. She nodded her head in agreement. Her eyes were closed so that she could better concentrate on the music.

The first piece ended. For a short moment there was a breathless quiet, then the crowd clapped. "Bravo! Bravo!" they called. All became silent again as the Maestro tapped the metal music stand.

"Ladies and gentlemen," he announced. "We are so glad you have come to the Song Fest. Welcome. Let me tell you a little about our Song Studio."

The Music Maestro seemed vaguely familiar. Where had they met before? The Ranger Leader studied the man's slender, trim form; there was something about him. . . .

"We have always felt that with so many Song Studios teaching the novice how to sing and make music, there was a need in Bright City for a studio to only teach the gifted musical artist. The music you hear today will not be like that in other Song Studios. It is finer. It is without mistake. It is the best you will hear. Music for the ear is also music for the heart. So all our sounds are the sweetest of sounds. And now I'd like to introduce a singer with one of the best voices in all the City. Oka! Let's give her a round of applause."

Thespia squeezed Hero's arm. There was a question in her eyes. Music was supposed to be for all the people. In all the Safe Places, apprentices learned to do their best, but for the sake of everyone, not for just a few. "Are these Kingsways?" she wondered aloud.

The people in the Song Studio applauded wildly for Oka. They stamped their feet. The lady in the chairs next to Hero suddenly stood, upturning a child who had been sitting on her lap. She hooted and hollered, "Oka! Oka!"

Above the clamor, Thespia, skilled indeed at monitoring the temper of audiences, shouted in Hero's ear, "She hasn't even sung yet! She must be wonderful."

Finally the Music Maestro struck the stand several times, and at last Oka came to the platform. Hero was surprised. Oka had always been rotund, and pleasantly so, but she must have put on fifty to eighty extra pounds! Why had this happened? Hero remembered her in Great Park. She had come hunting runaway orphans and wearing a large, round button that read: WE LOVE CHILDREN. Everyone knew what that meant: WE LOVE ORPHANS BECAUSE THEY DO OUR FORCED LABOR.

Oka was wearing a bright yellow dress that did nothing to hide her bulges. It was almost as though she was proud of being so heavy. The crowd quieted and settled into their seats. The lady on Hero's right sat back down on her two chairs.

The music of the instruments began, one flute and oboe and the violins playing the purest of sounds, the opening stanza a sweet prolonged strain of beautiful melody.

Oka waited for the introduction, then began to sing. Her voice was truly one of the most beautiful singing voices Hero and Thespia had ever heard. The people in the room became utterly subdued. The sound was so sweet that no one coughed, no one rustled in the chair, no one cleared a throat.

Hero closed his eyes and was lost himself for a while in this sweetest of sweetest sounds. Then he was prodded to attention by a sharp poke of Thespia's elbow in his side.

"Look," she whispered.

He opened his eyes and was amazed. Actual notes were coming out of Oka's mouth! The louder she sang, the more notes floated into the air. But they looked like—it couldn't be! It was! They were sweettreats. There were gingerbread eighth and quarter notes. There were lemon gumdrop whole notes. There were rests made of chocolate candy kisses.

As the sweetsounds floated over the heads of the audiences, people grabbed whatever note was above them. "Mine!" shouted the woman beside Hero, elbowing aside one of her own children. She stuffed her prize into her mouth as her children, who by now were standing on their own chairs, jumped to capture the floating candy notes.

The musicians kept playing, Oka went on singing, and the room was filled with the notes coming out of her mouth. People grabbed and pushed one another. They took more than they needed and didn't share with the persons beside them. *Who is listening to this beautiful music?* wondered Hero. As he watched the grabbing and feeding, he began to wonder if these people came to hear these sounds or just to eat them. No wonder everyone was so fat. No wonder Oka had gained so much weight. He had never been in a Song Fest where this had gone on.

The Music Maestro kept conducting, but glanced sideways over his shoulder every now and then at the sweetsound feeding that was going on. Each time he turned, he smiled at the crowd. Sure enough, he never grabbed a sweettreat for himself.

Again Hero was certain they had met somewhere before. But where could it have been?

"Hero!" Thespia whispered. She pointed to the Song Studio windows. On the outside were Lost Children pressing their noses to the glass, tapping with their skinny arms on the panes. They had gathered at the first sound of the orchestra, but now they stared, hunger in their eyes, at the feeding that was going on within. In one of his glances, the Music Maestro too noticed the outsiders. He waved his baton to an attendant. Hero and Thespia watched in surprise as the man closed and locked the Song Studio door.

Now Hero was angry. "Gather some of those gingerbread notes," he said. "How can these people stuff themselves when there are starving children standing outside?" He jumped from his seat and, pushing his way around the circle of chairs, hurried to a closed window and thrust it open.

At this the Maestro, still conducting, turned and saw what the Ranger Leader was doing. He motioned to the orchestra to keep playing and to Oka to keep singing, then rushed to stop Hero in his act.

"How dare you open the windows!" he said in a loud whisper. "These sweetnotes are only for those who really appreciate the sweetest of sounds. Lost Children don't know good music. They can't have our gingerbread quarter notes or our chocolate kiss rests."

By this time Thespia had gathered an armful of gumdrops and gingerbread. "Actually, Hero, don't give them too much. What these Lost Children really need is good nourishing food."

Hero took some of the sweettreats from her hands. The children could have something. How dare these people think the good music was for themselves alone! He wedged the window farther open and tossed the candy notes gently up and out, so they could be easily caught by the skinny hands outside, now upraised and grasping. "This will help them until our special assignment is finished. Then we can get them to Safe Places."

"No!" shouted the Music Maestro. "I will not have my good music wasted in the streets!"

At that, Thespia too became angry. The streets were the very place this beautiful music would do the most good. She loved to work in the streets of Bright City, bringing the King's stories to the most people. Drawing herself up to her most playerly stature, she spoke in a very loud stage voice, filling the room even above the orchestra and the singing. "Then why don't you invite the Lost Children in? They can hear the music inside and share in the goodies. In fact, let me go and bring them in."

The Music Maestro howled. "NOOOOO!" He turned to the audience, who were still stuffing their mouths with sweettreats as though there would be none tomorrow. "Do we want these dirty outsiders in our Song Studio?" he hollered.

Though their mouths were gooey with chocolate, and though they didn't stop eating for a moment, they shouted back, "NOOOOO! We don't want dirty outsiders in our Song Studio!"

Someone in the crowd yelled, "They'll eat all our sweetsounds!"

A flautist waved his instrument over his head and shouted, "They're too dirty. They only know street songs. They're not good enough for our Song Fest!"

Close up, Hero could see that when the crowd in the meeting room shouted out these words, a yellow light glittered in the eyes of the Maestro.

He cried, "Aha! This is my Song Studio. We will do here what I say!"

Suddenly Hero knew what was familiar about the man. He had seen impostors like this before. This was not a King's man. This was a saboteur, someone who had infiltrated a Safe Place and was actually teaching the people the Enchanter's ways. The Ranger Leader knew all too well the damage these evil fakirs could do. He slipped his hand to the handle of his hatchet.

At that, the Maestro hastened to the dais and interrupted the musicians and the singer. The music abruptly stopped. No more sweetsounds floated to the air to be grabbed and devoured by the audience.

"More music!" someone shouted.

"More sweetsounds!" cried another.

Children stood on their chairs and stamped their feet. A chant began to build. "MORE. MORE. MORE. MORE."

The Lost Children outside began to wail, "We want sweettreats. We want sweettreats."

Inside and outside a riot was building. Hero could see the yellow light glimmering in the eye of the Music Maestro, who turned with his hands upon his hips as if to say, "Now what are you going to do about it?" His eyes flashed forth more yellow glints. "What are you going to do? Start a riot?"

At this challenge, Hero began to unsheathe his hatchet. He was ready to go to arms right within the meeting room, no matter who got in harm's way.

At that moment, however, Thespia restrained his elbow. "Let me," she said. "I'm used to audiences." Without waiting for his approval, the Most Beautiful Player of All strode to the dais. Hero was amazed to see that she was applauding. "Bravo! Bravo!" he heard her call.

Confused, the audience stopped their demands.

Reaching the dais, Thespia quickly jumped up beside the Maestro, and before he could stop her, she drew Oka close. "Let's give a proper hand to these wonderful musicians."

The crowd applauded wildly. Maybe if they clapped enough the sweetsounds would begin again. Watching Thespia, Hero suddenly understood that facing any audience at any time was an act of courage.

Thespia raised her hands for silence and shot a dazzling smile that stunned the whole room into silence. How could they be rowdy in the face of such remarkable beauty?

"People!" Thespia called again. "People! We will continue the Song Fest, but first I thought you would like to know a little more about our gifted vocalist. Oka, you certainly have the most beautiful singing voice I have ever heard."

The people clapped again and pounded on their chairs. Without a doubt Oka's voice was the loveliest singing voice in the city. And she belonged to their Song Studio.

The Music Maestro watched Thespia. Hero could see that he was dumbfounded by her boldness. Hero himself was amazed by her easy command of the dangerous moment.

"Before you begin to sing again, Oka," the Player continued, "Tell us a little of your story. Once, I'm told, you used to be Orphan Keeper's Assistant. Is that right?"

Oka was not particularly pleased for everyone in the Song Studio to know this—but it was true. Yes, she had been Orphan Keeper's Assistant, and she had come from the Enchanted City to Great Park on an Orphan Hunt. In fact—in fact, that was where she had first met Hero. Oka wiggled her fingers at the Ranger Leader, still standing with his hand on the handle of his hatchet. He saluted her back.

And Oka giggled to remember the boy he had been. Smats and blats! Scarboy they had called him. And she recalled that they had once been friends, children really, together in Great Park, that wonderful land where everyone who hunted was welcome. And she remembered how unhappy she had been before she met Mercie. And that it was Mercie of Great Park who had taught her to sing around the cottage fireplace in order to sing her best in Great Celebration.

"And so it was Mercie who taught you how to sing," Thespia repeated as Oka told her story. "What else did Mercie teach you?"

It was then that Oka realized that something had gone wrong. For the first time she noticed the Lost Children, hungry and lonely, lined outside the Song Studio window, pressing their noses to the glass panes. The singer saw that none of them smiled. How unhappy they were! And she saw that the room was filled with fat people. Blats and smats! How had this happened? And she herself suddenly felt huge.

"Mercie taught me that—that in Great Park everyone belongs to someone else. Mercie taught me that—that to follow Kingsways meant giving every orphan a loving home."

What a wonderful idea! All the people in the audience sighed to think of it. Some of them had once been orphans. Some of them had once hidden in fearful hideaways. They forgot their longing for sweetsounds. And they began to wonder: How had everyone become so fat?

"Music! Music!" the Maestro shouted. He tapped on the stand to interrupt. Enough! Enough! Frantically, he lifted his baton to restore the enchantment that Thespia was breaking.

Thrum-m-m-m-m-m! Wham! The Maestro felt a tug at his cape. He staggered back, and the baton fell from his hand. Turning, he saw a silver-bladed hatchet pinning the hem of his silk-lined cape to the wooden floor of the dais.

In the light of the open window at the side of the meeting room, Hero now stood with his arms folded across his chest. "I think, Maestro, that you will be making no more music here." The Ranger Leader stuck his head out of the window, whistled, then called out, "TAXI!"

The sound of the Lost Children's cries echoed outside, "Taxi! Taxi!"

Thespia lifted her arms to the crowd again. She dazzled them with her smile. "The music in this Song Fest has grown a little too rich, don't you think?"

Yes, they did think it had become too sweet. They blinked their eyes as though waking from a kind of sleep. The lady sitting on two seats vowed that she was going on a diet starting that very minute.

"These are not Kingsways," the flautists and the oboist said in surprise to one another. Without a word they stood to their feet, put their instruments on their chairs, and grabbed the Maestro on either side, pinning his arms between them. "These are not Kingsways," they said to him. "Fine music is for all the people."

"Shall we open all the windows?" called out Hero, and the crowd in the meeting room shouted back, "Open all the windows." People rushed to throw them wide.

"Shall we invite the outsiders in?" the Ranger Leader asked again. And the people cried, "Kingsways! Kingsways! Bring the outsiders in!"

The Song Studio attendant unbolted the doors. He stepped outside and motioned to the crowd. Lost Children began to walk slowly, unbelievingly, into the studio. Were they really wanted here? They were so dirty, so skinny. People in the meeting room made places in the seats beside them. They motioned to empty spots on the floor nearest to the dais. As the newcomers found places, a violinist began to bow happy melodies, street songs the Lost Children loved.

Harnk! Harnk! a cabby tooted a horn at curbside.

Hero walked to the dais and with his strong arm jerked the hatchet from the floor. "You saboteur," he challenged. "You pretender. No more. No more. Everyone who loves music is welcome in any Song Studio. To the Garbage Dump with you."

The flautist and the oboist escorted the maestro pretender from the meeting room to the waiting taxi outside. And Hero called out to the crowded room with its open windows and open door, "Shall we begin the Song Fest again?"

The audience clapped their hands. "Begin again!" they cried back. "Begin again."

"And what songs will you sing, Oka?" Thespia asked.

Oka gave a deep sigh. What had been going on in here? She straightened her yellow dress. She really did need to take off some weight. Maybe a strolling street musician assignment would help. Oka remembered Mercie's cottage. She remembered the singing at Great Celebration. And she was sorry, suddenly sorry to have eaten so many of the sweetsounds herself. Clearing her throat, she announced, "I will sing all the King's Songs."

With that all the musicians began to play. Hero lifted a hand to Thespia to help her from the dais, so that in stepping down she would not trip over any of the Lost Children crowded on the floor.

Oka began to sing, and her notes dropped out of her mouth most wondrously. But now the people of the Song Studio made sure that the hungry ones got first pick and that the rest of the sweetsounds were collected in baskets to be taken through the city streets.

"I've had quite enough, thank you," they said to one another.

"Maybe we should take a few baskets to the Healing House," some decided.

"Good job," said Hero admiringly to Thespia as they stood together in the back of the Song Studio watching the amazing transformation. As usual, the King had known what he was doing.

When the player didn't answer, he said more. "I can't think of another city worker who could have done what you did. You knew exactly how to calm them, how to bring them to their senses. You were amazing, Thespia. And we worked very well together."

These were the sweetest words that Thespia could ever hear. She turned her dazzling smile on him, and in its light, a certain blindness of his own began to fade. Hero understood what Amanda had seen and what his younger brother had seen and what the King had known and had spoken to him that night of peril at Burning Place, "There is someone who loves you."

And looking down into the eyes of the Most Beautiful Player of All, Hero, like the audience, was instantly, absolutely dazzled.

The Great Celebration

"Oh, happy, happy," glowed the comet Demereaux, her tail scattering asteroid dust as she sped along the ellipse of her orbit. The King had appointed her his messenger to carry the news of Great Celebration, and Demereaux loved to be the bearer of good news. "To the Field of Stars," she called. "A marriage of Great Celebration is near."

Here in space, as well as in many other places, the King had much to do, but here his majesty blazed forth, here there were no disguises. His feet spanned a galaxy, a corona of light spangled his forehead, and starshine, like brilliants, dazzled in his eyes. He spun new moons and flung them forth. He cast fresh stars into the nighttime eons. When things were disappointing down below, solace was here in these acts of creation, and once spun into being, these created things stayed ordered. Here the Emperor of All, his Father, was close, and they wandered through the worlds together and talked of the wonder of the ways of heaven and of earth.

And now the wedding of his beloved friends was near. Another wobbling tilt of the world, and the Great Celebration would be at hand. All the celestial beings loved to bend near when happy ceremonies took place below. In readiness, wispy arches of the Milky Way had already draped themselves in the skies beyond the Field of Stars, and the twinkling hosts waited for the word that would gather them close.

"Time! Time!"

The King smiled as he heard Demereaux call out the good news. Here in celestial space there was no time, but always the endless stretching solicitude of being. Nevertheless, the heavenlies delighted in spying on earthtime. The comet came hurtling toward him, spangling the night with her enthused sparkling.

"Time! Time!"

The celestial ones all knew her cry summoned them to bend close for the wedding day.

"Demereaux!" the King called back in greeting. She spun around his head, dipped her tail, and then shot with accelerating velocity into the high night, sounding forth, "Ti-i-i-me!"

The King felt a sudden spacepulse. It was Pleiades. "M'Lord. M'Lord. Time. Time."

"Going now, Pleiades," said His Majesty. And with a tip of his hand to Ursa Minor, he was gone.

Down below, all Great Park was in a bustle with last-minute plans to welcome the citizens of Bright City within Stonegate Entrance. The aging knights, Sir Pumpkin and Sir Bumpkin, stood on either side of the path with their steeds poised grandly, just to give a little touch of chivalry to the affair. A troop of clown jugglers, trained by the best clown juggler of them all, practiced last minute tumbles and dives. Let no child here think that this wedding would be boring. In Great Park children never asked, "Mom, when is this going to be over?"

Flowers and herbs had been gathered in baskets for strewing. A bridal canopy had been set up on the ceremony site in the open spaces of the Practice Field. While bees practiced their best buzzing, birds ran through trilling scales. Striped tents had been pitched along forest paths and in meadows for overnight guests. Awnings sheltered the wedding tables in case of a slight afternoon rain shower, which Caretaker had predicted might take place.

"A pile of terry cloth towels for each guest," a young woman ordered her helpers. It was Cleone, once the girl named Dirty, now in charge of guest housekeeping. "And put some elbow grease into that!" Outside each tent, her helpers carefully placed a basin and bar of soap for those who wished to take a dip in the chill Duck Pond where even now waddling ducklings followed their mother for an early morning paddle.

Caretaker himself was splendidly garbed for this wedding. His white hair and beard had been freshly barbered, and he was up early tending to last-minute details in the Park. "Oh, happy day," he said as he danced along a meadow path. His pockets jingled with the sound of tools. Who knew what he might need for whatever emergency?

Stoneware jugs, beaded with sweat and filled with pressed cider, lined the banks of Lake Marmo where water and sand met and where the lapping edge cooled the beverage. Meanwhile, everyone agreed that the Chief Baker had outdone his own genius with towering baskets of still warm, yeasty fresh bread covered with white linen cloths. Brioches were ready, twisted braidloaves, melted cheese muffins and popovers. In the cool shadows of the storing cellar, the multi-tiered wedding cakes had been hidden, all golden with banana nut dough in the middle and rich with brown date dough on top.

Crews of Rangers pounded banner poles around the wedding site. Brilliant streamers were lifted by the wind and fluttered as bright heralds to the festivities. Eddie and Benji, the Powerworkers, were busy checking energy sources so that there would be nightlights for the evening festivities after the bridal pair had said their vows, cut the cakes, and were gone.

Since sunsleep, busy taxi vanguards had been shepherding city folk from Watchgate Entrance along the special road, cut for this festive occasion, which wound past the Garbage Dump. Bright Ones under King's command, usually away on royal assignments of protection, now guarded the edge of the refuse heaps to ensure that no dark thing breached any faultlines to corrupt the happiness of the day.

Two figures stood on the high ridge that overlooked all of Great Park. The sun had been up for an hour and was now glistening on the dew. Amanda and Hero stood side by side, their faces toward Deepest Forest, watching the mellow light of new day rising through the treeline. A floating wisp of smoke rose from the chimney of Mercie's Cottage.

"So," said Amanda, teasing just a little. "How goes this wedding morning for you?"

"It goes well." He heard the slight challenge in her voice. "And you were right, you know."

"Oh? Right about what?" Her voice rose. Amanda loved being right about anything.

"You were right about my—how did you put it?—my loving what I couldn't have and not loving what I could have which is far better for me than the love I did love."

She was silent, but without turning to look at her he knew the old insolent grin was on her face.

"Stop smirking." He pushed her side with a sharp jab of his elbow. Amanda particularly loved to be right when Hero was wrong.

At that moment the Ranger horns blasted, *"Croiee! Croiee!"* and the morning watch cried, "All goes well! The world goes well!" He suddenly remembered the time when a faithless ranger had set fires in the forest, and the two of them, children still, had struggled alongside the firefighters cutting breaches in the underbrush and setting backfires. Hero recalled how terrified he had been of the flames.

"Amanda?" She was silent, but he continued, "Because you were right, just to make me feel better about you always being so right, I wonder if you would give me a gift? A boon, a bridegroom boon, please, for my marriage day?"

She laughed finally, and faced him, and he remembered how often one heard Amanda before seeing her.

"Any gift, if I can, Bridegroom, sir. But hurry before I change my mind."

He turned, faced her, and took her hand. "Friendship. That's all. Promise me your lasting friendship."

The horns blared again. It was time for Hero to return to Ranger Command Post, there to make ready and to wait for the King and the wedding merrymakers.

"Gotta go," he said and turned, but she caught him and grasped his hand in the Ranger clasp, and this time she moved quickly, tucked her foot behind his ankle, and tripped him.

Bested again! Lying low, he grabbed her ankle, but she was laughing so loudly, he could not help but laugh along.

"Friendship," she gasped between chortles. "That I can give and have always given you. Gladly. For old and good time's sake."

Croiee! Croiee! With that blast, Hero was up and off. Midafternoon high would be near soon enough, and running down the trail he could still hear Amanda laughing. And it gladdened him and seemed to gladden the already happy world.

In Mercie's Cottage, Thespia was almost ready. Her dress, bright with gold and plum and crimson stripe, was low in the bodice and puffed in the sleeves above her elbows. The blouse of the dress was ruched and tucked, gathered at the waistline which flared in a graceful circle to the hem. A posy of winding ivy and lilies tied with streaming satin ribbons waited in a white ironstone pitcher.

When Amanda entered, Mercie was just placing the bride's garland on Thespia's full and curling strawberry blonde hair. Beautiful as the player was, she had never been more beautiful than at this moment as a bride.

"Like it?" She turned, her satin ballet slippers just showing beneath the skirt. Her eyes shone.

The Princess nodded her head in approval and clapped her hands. She had always loved Thespia.

"And how is the bridegroom this morning?" Mercie asked.

"You mean Hero?" Amanda responded, as though there could be another.

"I mean my boy." Mercie tied the ribbons at the back of the bride's dress.

Amanda laughed. "They're all your boys. This one is glad on this wedding morning. In fact, I've never seen him so glad."

Thespia smiled radiantly.

Croi-Croi! Croi-Croi! The King. The King was at the gates.

Thespia ran to the cottage door and made sure the children were not so engrossed in playing catch and tag that they forgot to take up the baskets of petals. "Children!" she cried. "Children!"

The path from Stonegate Entrance was already adrift with flowers and lined with guests who had come to accompany His Majesty's party to Ranger Command Post and then to Mercie's Cottage and then to the ceremony site.

Mandolin players, lutists, and drum beaters struck their song as soon as the King came into view. He was dressed in an open shirt gathered at the neck and wrists, with a blue Ranger sash crisscrossing his breast. His dun pants were tucked into dress Ranger boots.

"The King! The King!" the people cried as he passed. His eyes still held the spangle of starshine. As he passed through the crowd, he swooped a small child up and placed him on his broad shoulders.

The young men with the King marched along the path, catching the hands of the maidens and stepping for a moment with them in time to the music of the songsters. Boys did handsprings and cartwheels as the procession journeyed on. A young woman began to sing "The Song of the King." From watchtower to watchtower the song echoed. Cooks putting joints into ovens and women still gathering herbs for strewing and the bride waiting for her bridegroom all heard the glad words and began to sing along.

The King is always with you,
In battle, at your hind side,
In duty, at your working hand,
In sleep, protecting o'er you.

In love he is your heartsong,
The King. The King.

The procession came to Ranger Command Post. "Is there a Bridegroom ready? Or is he still in bed?"

Hero came to the door, tall in Ranger dress blues. "I'm not sleeping!"

White-haired Caretaker was at one side, beaming in his role as a groomsman, and on the other side was the bridegroom's brother, Hunter.

"Yo!" someone shouted, and the three started with the sound of the tambourine and the beat of the drum up the path, followed by the wedding procession, to Mercie's Cottage to collect the bride.

"A wedding! A wedding!" children cried, not forgetting their jobs. From the baskets over their arms they strewed flowers and fragrant herbs and leaves of low growing plants along the path before the bridegroom to the gate of Mercie's Cottage.

Here the King cried again, "Is there a Bride ready?"

And Thespia appeared, glowing, with Mercie on one side, her white hair curling beneath her snood, and Amanda on the other, gowned in bride's colors, each beautiful in her own way.

"Your Majesty," the three said together and curtsied low.

The young men in the wedding party clapped, the tambourines jangled, and Hero stepped forth to take the hand of the one who would promise to stay beside him for life.

The guests had gathered on the Practice Field and waited until the Bride and Groom and the Wedding Procession halted beneath the canopy.

"Isn't she beautiful, Ruthie?" whispered a little grandma to her good friend, who whispered back, "Just lovely, Sarah, sweetie. A beautiful bride."

The King lifted his hands to hush the crowd as a trumpeter blew a cadence. When all was still, the King's voice could be heard, strong and clear, above the heads of all the wedding guests. "Let the Celebration begin!"

Tenderly Hero took his Bride's hand as together they repeated the wedding vows.

In the crowd, Oka fished a handkerchief out of her bag and blew her nose. "Such a handsome pair!" she said under her breath. "Oh, I just love weddings."

Then the King turned toward the newlywed couple and said with a wink, "I think you're going to like this." He lifted his hands and cried, "Time!"

The skies darkened just slightly, readying for Caretaker's afternoon shower, just enough to cool things a little. And then the meteors soared through space. Planets bobbled slightly to tip greetings to the pair who loved. Satellites flared forth in rounding parabolas. Showers of meteorites blazed. Constellations winked in symmetry, then blinked again.

Then from the crowd, a shout went forth. Taxis outside the gate honked. The Bridegroom had kissed his Bride! And dancing and singing, the wedding guests greeted one another and agreed it had been the best wedding they had ever attended. The people of Bright City joined the people of Great Park. Heaven bent near to earth. And best of all, the King himself was at Celebration.

"Oh, happy! Happy!" shimmered Demereaux as she shot along the ellipses of the sky. "Oh, happy, happy day!"